TAKING CHARGE OF YOUR TEAM

EMBASSY BOOKS
www.embassybooks.in

Taking Charge Of Your TEAM

Published in India by :
Embassy Books in Association with Knowledge Partner
Global Success University,
120, Great Western Building,
Maharashtra Chamber of Commerce Lane,
Kala Ghoda, Fort,
Mumbai- 400 023.
Tel : (+91-22) 22819546 / 32967415
Email : info@embassybooks.in
www.embassybooks.in

ISBN : 978-93-85492-61-7

CONTENTS

PREFACE

Recap your life up to this moment. On how many occasions were you alone, and how many times were you surrounded by people? Surviving in this world is a team game.

Humans are referred to as social animals for a reason. We need each other for survival. Life is not an individual endeavour; it is a journey that is shared with others. We have companions at various stages of our life. Even without us realizing it, we work in teams. Apart from a formal team at our workplace, we frequently deal with informal teams like our friends, family, relatives, neighbours, clubs, etc. Team building and team management is therefore essential not only in our professional lives, but also to manage our personal lives efficiently.

If you believe that 'I' is the most powerful alphabet then do not read beyond this point. The word 'TEAM' does not have an 'I'. 'TEAM' stands for 'Together Everyone Achieves More' and there is no scope for the 'I' attitude. This book highlights the 'We' attitude and helps to curb the crab mentality.

The purpose of this book is to empower you with the wisdom to lead your life and your team towards your goals. This book is a guide to warn you about the perils of mismanagement and showcase strategies that will help you to maximise your team's potential. It is a culmination of thoughts and ideas, which when implemented will allow you to optimise your team's resources and channelize the energies towards success.

What Can You Derive From This Book?

This book is a means to an end. The end you have always dreamt about. The end in which you see yourself as an efficient ruler, expanding your empire with a strong and resourceful team. The end in which you and your team achieve the ultimate goal.

This book is aimed to help you in every stage of the dream you envision for your team. Each chapter in this book is designed for robust team building and management. These ten chapters will escort you in your journey to become an excellent team leader and a manager. With stories, anecdotes, exercises and theories, this book will equip you to handle any dreadful situation faced by your team in a tactful manner.

The journey starts with teaching you ways to lay a strong foundation. It moves on to educate you about team development, team dynamics and introduce you to distinct team personalities. The book throws light upon sound communication strategies and effective task delegation. You can also learn to motivate, empower, resolve conflicts and reward your team for their efforts.

How to Use This Book?

This book is your friend, philosopher and guide. It lays down a clear path and at times shouts out to instil in you the right skill required to be a successful team player, manager and a leader. The simple stories and anecdotes will inspire you and encourage you to look at life from a different perspective. This book is a one-time investment but certainly not a one-time read. Go through this book chapter-wise and mark the sections that you feel exactly apply to you and will help you improve.

As you browse through the book, you may realise that at some point in your life, you have faced similar situations. Once you read the whole book, you can revisit certain sections and draw parallels between your situation and the situations mentioned in the chapters. Apply the given model to it. You will be able to determine the difference it would have made to that particular situation. This will not only help you identify areas of improvement but also provide you techniques to achieve the same.

You can also return to individual chapters, as and when you require help for any issues in your team. Make notes as and when you come across something you feel you need to work on.

You will be a part of various teams throughout your life. Every team needs a good player, a great manger and an inspiring leader. Read this book and apply the strategies mentioned in it to efficiently manage and *take charge of your team.*

"Whenever the mind of man can conceive and believe, the mind can achieve."

- Napoleon Hill

CHAPTER 1

THE FOUNDATION

The Mountain Gate

Several years ago, a traveller was trekking in the snow-clad Himalayan Mountains. Having scaled a few peaks, he rested and drank hot tea. While he was sipping the refreshing beverage, he overheard a few locals speak about a mystical gate called Mountain Gate. The adventurer in him could not resist overhearing the mesmerising conversation. From the discussion, he gathered that Mountain Gate was some kind of a portal to the afterlife. His curiosity piqued.

He eagerly listened to their conversation and made a note of the route that a local claimed would take someone to the mysterious Mountain Gate. Draped in a fur coat and armed with a strong stick, the traveller ventured towards the Mountain Gate. The journey was scenic but challenging. He battled the chilly wind and sneaked through slippery creeks. He scaled the mighty mountain and the treacherous paths with sheer determination and crossed it to reach a cave. As he stooped to enter the cave, he saw a narrow passage with light at the other end. He slowly approached the light. Suddenly, he could feel a change in the temperature. The chills were replaced by warmth and the weather turned pleasant.

The traveller sneaked passed the narrow inlet and reached the other side where a chubby little girl greeted him. She offered the traveller some refreshments and congratulated him on reaching the Mountain Gate. The girl then led the traveller to two doors. The traveller opened the squeaky door of the first room and saw six old people sitting at a table staring at a bowl of rice. They all looked frail and weak. The bowl of rice was full; they were equipped with spoons as well. But they couldn't eat. The handle of the spoon was larger than their arms. They were unable to place the spoon in their mouths.

Alarmed by the plight of the six people, the traveller chose to open the second door. To his amazement, the other room also housed six people at a table with a bowl of rice in front of them. Their spoons also had those long handles but these people looked healthy and cheerful.

The traveller was dumbfounded and asked the little girl what was happening. The little girl explained to the traveller that the first room was hell while the second room was heaven. The people in the second room fed each other with the spoons. People were so greedy in the first room that they starved, while people in the second room believed in teamwork and fed each other.

From 'I' to 'We'

Team building and management is extremely crucial for the long-term success of any organisation or a relationship. It provides a boost to the organisation and fosters productivity. Over the years, individuals and organisations have realised the value of team building.

1.   Target Practice

The most important attribute of successful team building is that everybody is oriented towards his/her goal. The efforts of each member would then be channelized to achieve the ultimate objective of the team or the organisation. Many people consider goal-oriented behaviour as an inherent quality; but they are wrong. People have different agendas, governed by selfish desires. Sound team-building activities help eradicate the team members from the captivity of pessimism and move towards the positive path. It will ensure that each team player is clear about his/her targets, leading to enhanced productivity.

2. Get well

Lack of communication within teams is a major concern. Communication helps people share ideas and maintain an identical thought process. It makes sure that everybody is thinking along the same lines, and that time and energy are not being wasted on vague ideas. Communication enables people to follow clear instructions and know their role in the bigger scheme of things. Team building makes it easy to coordinate. Precious time and energy is saved in the process. Effective communication helps resolve conflicts smartly and come up with the ideal solution. Sound communication reduces arguments and results in amicable relationships.

3. Curb the Crab Mortality

Trusting people is often an impediment when people approach a situation in a group. Team building needs people to trust each other. Trust provides the motivation to team members to perform. It also teaches the members to put the team ahead of themselves. The crab mentality is curbed and people start helping each other, when they start trusting. Everyone puts in their best effort, not to gain mileage over others but to help each other accomplish their goal.

By inculcating strong team building values in a team, what one member lacks, the other members can contribute, forming a symbiotic relationship. Team members strive hard not to let their team down. They take care of each other and invariably take care of themselves in the process. Their thought process changes from 'I' to 'We'. Team members are motivated and dedicated towards the progress of the team. It results in increased productivity and goal accomplishment.

Two Sides of the Same Coin

Management and leadership need to go hand-in-hand if one has to achieve the goal. They are two sides of the same coin and have their differences as well as similarities. A team requires a manger as well as a leader. Can both the roles be performed by one person? The answer is a resounding yes!

Let's see what defines a leader and a manager:

- A Leader inspires the team to move towards a vision. A Manager makes sure that the team works smoothly to achieve that vision.

- A Leader commands respect, a Manger demands it.

- A Leader is associated with development, while a Manager deals with maintenance.

- A Leader concentrates on people and a Manger concentrates on systems.

- Leadership is based on trust, Management is based on control.

- A Leader deals with long-term strategies, a Manager handles short-term strategies.

- The Leader looks at the horizon, while a Manager looks at the bottom line.

During the Industrial Age, these two aspects could easily be separated. However, in this Information Age, it is not only difficult, but also detrimental to a company's success to separate these two aspects. In the earlier era, a manger was looked upon as a taskmaster. One who assigned tasks to workers and made sure that they performed them. The focus was on efficiency. Today's era deals with value creation using knowledge. Workers look to their managers, not just for assigning tasks, but also for inspiration and a sense of purpose.

The person handling the team needs to be a good leader as well as a manger. Both the positions have their own set of challenges. When it comes to controlling and coordinating the activities of a group to further the organisation's pursuit of achieving its goals, both these roles must be adequately balanced. Leadership and management are not exclusive; they are mutually beneficial.

Sometimes, leaders assume the role of a manager and vice versa. Managers tend to follow the leader's vision and align the team members towards it. In doing so, they also assume the role of a leader at some level. Leaders cannot distinguish themselves from the team members, they need to mingle with the crowd and engage in mundane activities sometimes.

If you are looking to take charge of your team, then the challenge is to lead your team to a vision and manage the day-to-day operations so that you reach your collective goal. Maintaining the right balance between management and leadership will provide you with the competitive advantage required to ace at the top level.

> Maintaining the right balance between management and leadership will provide you with the competitive advantage required to ace at the top level.

Ten Avatars of a Manager

We know team building and management requires the team leader or the manager to shift between roles. Henry Mintzberg had identified major roles that a manager needs to play, to take charge of the team and achieve the goal. The ten roles in an organisational context are as follows:

1. Figurehead:

As the person in charge of a team, there are social and legal responsibilities that one needs to take care of. Leaders need to inspire people to achieve their task, as people look up to the person in that position for guidance.

You are a figurehead, an authoritative figure, meant to walk the talk. Under this role, you will have to be a symbolic leader. You represent your team and need to project the right image. Be aware of your behaviour and reputation as every step will be monitored. You need to be a good role model for others to follow suit.

2. Leader:

Leader does not necessarily mean the CEO of the company. One can be a leader of a team or a department. This role requires you to guide and mentor your team towards success. Show them the path and inspire them to continue on it by motivating the team members from time to time.

This role requires you to engage in productive conversations with team members. You need to concentrate on building your emotional intelligence. This position commands respect and people will only respect you if you are worthy of it.

3.   Liaison:

This role demands that one communicates on behalf of the team with others. Everyone perceives the world in a different manner. This is where communication is of vital importance.

As a liaison, you need to communicate effectively with everyone involved so that all of you are on the same page, and be in touch with your internal as well as external contacts. You need to excel at business correspondence, participate in meetings with other leaders and share the information with your team. You need to sharpen your networking skills for this role.

4.   Monitor:

Keeping a close eye on the environment will allow you to change quickly without any hindrance. Monitoring is necessary to stay abreast of the changes in internal

> Keeping a close eye on the environment will allow you to change quickly without any hindrance.

and external environment, so that you can adapt to those changes efficiently. Monitor your team to make a note of their productivity and help them enhance their performance.

You will be required to seek and access official information. You have to attend industry-specific seminars and conferences to stay in touch with the latest offerings. You need to hone your analytical skills to monitor the happenings effectively.

5.   Disseminator:

As a disseminator, you are expected to communicate your learning to your team. Your colleagues look up to you as a trusted source of information and you need to live up to that reputation.

In this role, you communicate useful information to your colleagues, which will ease their task and provide them with some clarity regarding it. You will be disseminating information to others within the organisation. Develop your communication skills to ace as a team leader or manager.

6.   Spokesperson:

As a disseminator you communicated internally, as a spokesperson, you will be communicating externally. You represent your team or your organisation while communicating with the outside world. In this role, you will be transmitting information to the outside world. Spokespersons work with the media and make sure that the team is represented appropriately.

As a spokesperson of your team, you will be attending external meetings and conferences and reporting the progress of your team or organisation. You have to choose your words wisely.

7.   Entrepreneur:

Entrepreneurs drive ideation. You will innovate and improve projects. You will forecast the future and plan for it accordingly. You will be creating and controlling change in your organisation. People will expect you to solve problems with optimal solutions.

In order to excel at your role as an entrepreneur, you will have to master the art of change management. People often fear change. In an organisational set up, change is inevitable. The sooner your team is prepared for the change the easier it will be to deal with it.

8.   Disturbance handler:

A team comprises of different people and different people think differently. When people perceive the same things differently, it results in a conflict. As a team leader, you will have to listen to the grievances of your team and resolve their conflict. Many times, you will have to manage the emotions within your team by being in control of your emotions.

Disturbances take place externally as well. You need to be tactful in dealing with external forces. You will have to understand the core problem and take corrective measures that will suit the conflicting parties. As a disturbance handler, your job will be to manage any sort of crisis faced by the team.

9.   Resource allocator:

Optimum utilisation of resources is a manger's success mantra. You will have to figure out ways and means to use the organisations resources tactfully. The resources range from manpower to finance. Scheduling, budgeting and prioritising skills are necessary to be a good resource allocator.

10.   Negotiator:

A negotiator makes sure that every party benefits from the deal. A leader is a part of important negotiations involving your team and the organisation at large. You will have to defend the business interest by actively participating in negotiations.

A strong team manager is the foundation of a strong team. All these ten roles are interlinked. A manager needs to maintain a balance between these ten avatars, changing swiftly and adapting to the role quickly.

If you want to know how you face in the ten avatars, go ahead and rate your performance for every avatar on a scale of one to five. Count your heads!

Locker Room and Boardroom

Whenever we speak about team building, managers and leadership, one topic is bound to come up along with the organisational aspect – Sports. The boardroom and the locker room may seem poles apart but the common link between the two is team building. Winning teams in sports and business have a lot in common.

When people work together, the result is often in their favour. People who are working towards the same goal must be like-minded and in synchronisation with one another. An individual can derail the hopes of success. A sports star working alone can miss an easy goal-scoring opportunity, while a trader without his team might goof up trading a major stock. The contribution of every teammate is important. However, some with greater potential must contribute more than the others. The CEO of a company has more power and potential than a supervisor working in the same company. Similarly, in a sports scenario, the captain, the star player and the manager have more power and potential to change the game. Everyone must contribute according to his/her individual capacity for the team to succeed.

> Everyone must contribute according to his/her individual capacity for the team to succeed.

The four P's Formula is applicable to organisations as well as sports teams. The four P's stand for: People, Personality, Process and Purpose. It is imperative to choose the right people, shape their personality, follow a stringent process and work towards achieving the purpose of the team. Having star performers stocked in your team won't guarantee you a win unless they play together as a team. They need to have a sound leader to guide them. Just like a sports team, a successful sales force also needs to be directed towards a vision. They also need to follow a strategy.

Often, it is about having the right people at the right place. You cannot expect results if you place a defender in place of an attacker in football, and place a human resource person in charge of handling operations. Minute details should be checked. Just like athletes time and monitor their progress, every team must analyse the performance of its team members. Practice is crucial for delivering the perfect sales pitch as well as scoring a free kick. Preparation conditions your mind for success. This helps you to not become overwhelmed by the situation and stay calm and composed in pressure situations.

> Preparation conditions your mind for success.

Sports teams play a lot of tournaments in a season. Aiming to win a tournament is similar to aiming to excel in the financial quarter. Your team's performance in the tournaments and quarters will ultimately decide your team's fate in the season and the financial year, respectively.

Sports results in instant gratification, whereas you have to wait for a long while in business to taste success. However, the importance of strategies, planning and execution remains the same in both cases. You have to build a strong foundation before gaining momentum, knocking-off your opponent and continuing with your juggernaut.

Chapter Rewind

1. Team building and team management are essential not only in our professional lines, but also to manage our personal lives efficiently.

2. Leadership and management are not exclusive, they are mutually beneficial.

3. Ten avatars of a manager's are ten roles expected of them.

4. Optimum utilisation of resources is a manager's success mantra.

5. A strong team manager is the foundation of a strong team.

6. The right time is now or never.

7. The only thing that is constant in this world is change and everybody fears change. Don't fear change; befriend it.

8. Be strong, if you don't stand for something, you will fall for anything.

9. If you don't have a proper foundation in life, it is bound to go wrong.

"I cannot change the direction of the wind but I can adjust my sails to always reach my destination."

– Jimmy Dean

CHAPTER 2

TEAM DEVELOPMENT

The English Debacle

English football fans were highly excited for the 2010 FIFA World Cup. There were huge expectations from the team but it failed to live up to them. The team's poor performance was attributed to a host of problems. They had fundamental problems that prevented the team from accomplishing their goals.

The English Premier League is considered the talent pool from which the national team is chosen. This structure faced a lot of flak for the dismal performance of the national team at the World Cup.

Clubs that are mostly foreign-owned entities dominate the Premiership. They look at the Premiership as a business venture and are not too concerned about the performance of the national team. They feature a lot of foreign stars, and as a result, the budding players do not get adequate opportunity to showcase their talent and gain experience at the big level.

Clubs are profit-driven entities and are constantly on the lookout for commercial partnerships. Players are forced to play a lot of matches in a short duration, which results in a burn out. Moreover, the international tournament takes place in the one-month window that is generally the resting period for the footballers.

However, the Premiership cannot be solely blamed for the debacle. The body governing the game in England also went through a rough patch leading up to the tournament. They had to face resignations and scandals that created a negative impact. The team's coach also had a communication problem with the players. The incentives of salary and the coach of the national team were not aligned to performance. Commercialisation of the game had crippled the foundation of the national squad.

All these problems would still have surfaced if the England football team had performed well at the World Cup. It was just a ticking time bomb waiting to explode. A team's performance depends on intrinsic as well as extrinsic factors. Misalignment at the foundation level can topple the entire structure. Teams need to be developed from the core and it needs to be strengthened before adding another layer. The team development process needs to be followed strictly and reviewed from time-to-time for a team's success.

> Teams need to be developed from the core and it needs to be strengthened before adding another layer.

The team development process of the English football team was flawed at various levels and as a result, they had to suffer its consequences.

The Story of a Team

A team is a sum of individuals. They come together to achieve a common goal. Initially, every individual looks to gain personal advantage and the team is not given much importance. This is mainly because the tasks are individualistic and the teammates do not know each other.

Gradually, team members start interacting with each other, either due to the nature of the task or due to personal liking. These relationships are often established for personal gain. Once the task is completed, the team member goes back to their individualistic approach.

The team gels well when they share a common purpose. Each member works in unison when the team is in pursuit of a goal that can only be achieved through teamwork. The goal should motivate the team members and appeal to their emotions. Each member must be possessed by the idea of achieving the goal. At this stage, team members put the team ahead of themselves. They do this when they realise that greater things can be achieved by working together rather than working individually. A bond is created between team members and they start sharing their thoughts and ideas with each other. Teams that perform together achieve lot more than teams that work on an individualistic approach.

Greater things can be achieved by working together rather than working individually.

Once the team members get comfortable with each other, achieving goals becomes relatively easier. The team can venture into unknown territory and explore lucrative opportunities. They have the confidence to face uncertainties because of their bonding. It acts as a shield against negativity and propels the team to aspire for more.

The Birth of the Champions

Let's explore the evolution of a champion team in detail with the help of the Tuckman's model. The model states that every team passes through four stages: Forming, Storming, Norming and Performing. These phases are necessary for the development of the team. Throughout yours lifetime, you must have been a part of some team or the others. While reading the following process, you can relate to your experience and draw parallels to get a grasp of the situation.

1.   Forming

Forming is the stage where the team is assembled. In this stage, team members are unaware of each other's roles as well as their own role at this stage. They try to establish base level expectations. Few people make an effort to bond with each other. Some agree on common goals and function accordingly. Attempts are made to develop trust.

Individuals are not aware about the exact functioning of the team. Not all the members endorse the mission completely. There are doubts in everyone's mind regarding the future course of action. There is plenty of scope to learn. The group is quite new and does not have a history. The team members are not yet fully committed to the goal.

At this stage, the team members look for some clarity of thought. Your role as a manger is to set a mission for the team. You must clearly explain how you aim to achieve the common goal. You have to assign roles to the members so that they know how they are going to contribute to the task. It is important to move out of the initial phase and establish a protocol.

You must establish a reward structure so that the team members know what they are working towards. You must ensure that the team members are committed to the task and ask them to take a call regarding their dedication towards the task.

2.   Storming

In this stage, the team members settle in their role. They look for power and control. They develop their communication skills and start identifying resources that will help them in the long run. They react to leadership and express themselves freely.

The members are well aware of their roles and responsibilities and they work relentlessly towards the agenda. Everyone has an opinion; this delays decision-making and problem-solving process. This stage witnesses the formation of groups within a group. The competition level rises and team spirit takes a hit. A lot of personal attacks are made, which either spurs the members to perform to their potential or prompts them to submit meekly.

As the team leader, you should take control in such a situation and reinforce the positive environment that prevailed earlier. You should support your team members and acknowledge their efforts without any bias. You must encourage feedback and build trust. This is the make-or-break phase. Every team will pass through this; the important thing to consider here is that only teams that have the patience and the maturity would grow past it.

3. Norming

The storm has passed and the situation is back to normal at this stage. Members agree about roles and processes for problem solving. Decisions are made through negotiation and consensus building. Team members trust each other and believe in each other's capabilities. There is a healthy competition, and creativity is encouraged. There are no hidden agendas and everybody works to accomplish the ultimate goal. All the members are committed and work to their potential. The teammates are comfortable with each other's working style and share responsibility accordingly.

The team members communicate all the time, and constantly work towards improving each other's performance. The team has one goal and a mutual plan to achieve it. People endorse each other's ideas and avoid conflicts. The only issue at this stage is that members may tend to shy away from pointing out the drawbacks of an idea to avoid conflict.

Your role as the team leader demands that you bring to the table both the good things and the bad things. You can indulge in constructive criticism and motivate your team to conquer the drawbacks and proceed towards the goal.

> Your role as the team leader demands that you bring to the table both the good things and the bad things.

4. Performing

The team members perform to their potential and achieve the target they set for the team. They work collaboratively and care about each other's well being. They possess a great team spirit and it gets reflected in their performance.

The manager plays a passive role at this stage. The team is self-motivated and conducts operations efficiently. The members feel attached to the team and are willing to sacrifice for the team's wellbeing. Team members are competent, autonomous and handle the decision-making process amicably and with ease. Everything culminates into superior team performance.

Teams pass through these stages over and over again. A change in circumstances propels the cycle to go back to a previous stage. For example, a change in leadership or new workforce can send the development process back to the Storming Stage. In order to take charge of your team at various levels, you have to act according to the situation. You have to be tactful in your approach and react according to the development phase of your teams.

Time to Assemble

Pick out any successful team of your choice. It can be a sports team, business team or a team from any other sector. If you look closely at these successful teams, you will find that they are not stashed with superstars. There might be certain players on whom the team relies more, but the team's success depends on the balance. The managers or the team leader's job is to maintain this balance. Your job is to ensure that the team's engine is well oiled and functions at an optimum level. Here are some steps that will guide you to build an effective and cohesive team.

1.   Set the Destination

Streamline your team members' efforts by conveying the exact goal to them. Providing them a well-defined purpose will help channelize their energies effectively. When everyone knows where they are going, it makes the journey a lot easier.

Mangers take it for granted that since people are working in an organization for a considerable amount of time, they know about their objectives and importance. What they do not understand is that the team members are constantly looking out for validation.

Team members need to know whether they are doing the right things and have a chance to grow within the organisation. These are the questions that remain unanswered. They never ask them, so no one ever tells them. This hurdle can be easily crossed if the team leader communicates effectively with the team members and explains them their role and the benefits associated with it.

2. Define Who's Who

Explain to your team members how their contribution is going to add value to the company's goal. They must understand their role in order to perform effectively. A striker in a football game needs to know that his job is to look for goal scoring opportunities without considering the defence strategies. His job is to score goals, which will eventually lead to a team victory.

A Broadway musical is a perfect example of synchronisation. Every artist knows his/her role and performs it without worrying about anything else. This does not mean that the dancers do not care about the musicians. It means that everyone concentrates on his/her individual task so that the output is something spectacular.

3. Talk. Listen. Communicate

Workers work in alienation in illegal bomb-manufacturing units. Some department works on the outer shell of the bomb while the other works on the pin. They do not know that they are contributing in making bombs. To them, they are manufacturing pins and outer shells. Do not use the bomb factory approach while managing your team.

An organisation has many departments and it is important to make sure that these departments communicate with each other for a better final product. The changes made in one process need to be communicated to the other departments for maintaining continuity. Ensure that your team members stay in touch with each other, especially with members who work on the extension of their task.

4. Be wary of Groups within Groups

Keep an eye on teams within teams. It is natural for individuals to take a liking towards few people in a team. There might be dislikes as well. This leads to the creation of internal groups. Such groups within a team can have both positive and negative impacts on the team. On a positive level, people can bond better and develop friendship but on a negative level, few people can feel left out of the team and this can be detrimental to the overall team spirit.

5.   Conflict Management

Conflicts may arise between groups or individuals. It is natural for conflicts to arise when people are working in a group, as everyone has a different mindset. Conflicts, if dealt with properly can generate constructive ideas and motivate the team. As a manager, it is important for you to anticipate retaliation and be prepared to resolve a conflict constructively.

You cannot avoid or ignore conflicts but you can manage them. You should deal with the situation tactfully without hurting anyone's feelings or being biased. Listen to everyone's grievances before coming to a conclusion. You cannot follow one method to resolve all types of conflicts. Your approach should depend upon the nature of the conflict and the people involved in the conflict.

> Conflicts, if dealt with properly can generate constructive ideas and motivate the team.

Eventually, you need to empower your team members to resolve their own conflicts. Create a framework that will resolve conflicts amicably. That said, do not try to be their agony aunt. You have a department to run and if you get involved in your team members' petty problems, it is going to go downhill for you.

6.   Captain the Team

Do not forget that you are the captain of the ship. You need to be in command so that your voyage reaches its destination in time. If you are involved in activities like cleaning the deck, preparing food for the crew and managing the sails, then who is going to manage your team? You cannot be in all the places at once, so you have to entrust others to do their job and back their abilities.

Your job is to assign the right person for cleaning the deck, prepare the food and manage the sails. You only need to supervise your team members and not perform their task. Lead the way for others to follow. Efficient delegation and management would not only get all the things done, but it would help you achieve that within the prescribed time and resources.

7.   Connect

Meetings are essential to stay on track. You must encourage your team members to speak at meetings. Each member has a different background and a different orientation. Everyone can bring something new to the table. You must give each team member a fair chance to voice his/her opinion.

Do not play the role of a teacher at a meeting. Your team members should interact with each other. They must not channelize everything through you. Such a situation might result in unhealthy competition and one-upmanship. It is vital to build synergy for the team's success. Team synergy helps foster creativity and innovation.

8.   Receive

Team members are in your team because they are qualified to be there. They have the required skill set, which can be utilised in an efficient manner if their inputs are also taken into consideration. You can let your team members be flexible in choosing their approach towards a particular task. Give them a deadline and the freedom to function according to their approach.

Encourage them to give suggestions. An experienced cook has a mastery over his art and can provide invaluable suggestions to improve your dish. Provide your team members with adequate feedback and let them know when their suggestions are implemented.

9.   Counter Head Mentality

Successful teams can easily slip into the herd mentality. Often, this is what lets them down in the long run. When teams are performing well, you may have a few members, who suppress their thoughts and do not contribute in giving suggestions when their suggestions contradict the majority. They would agree with the views expressed in meetings just because the majority has agreed on them. This is a major impediment for innovation, and a team that does not innovate, fails in the long run.

You must also make room for minority and unpopular views. The team members must feel confident to speak up and voice their opinion.

10. Celebrate

Acknowledge your team's efforts by celebrating when your team reaches milestones. Incremental acknowledgements are better than appreciating the team after the completion of the task. Incremental appreciation keeps the team motivated. Small celebrations and team building activities are a must to inculcate team spirit.

Eventually, you want your team members to look out for each other. Team members need to look at each other as allies and not as enemies. Team spirit acts as an additional player on your side, which is often the difference between winning and losing.

11. Criticise Constructively

You must give individual feedback to your team members to help them grow. Feedback is not necessarily negative. Mangers take it for granted that no negative feedback is positive feedback. No, you need to convey negative as well as positive feedback.

Just as incremental appreciation fosters team spirit, feedback also builds individual morale. The team member knows that he/she is on the right track and continues to function effectively when given a positive feedback. Team members should also indulge in constructive criticism of each other's work.

12. Recognize. Acknowledge. Reward

Acknowledge team as well individual successes and let everybody know about the feat. Specify the details and the roles that each member played to accomplish the goal. Explain how the team overcame challenges and succeeded. Mention each and everyone in the group.

Do not forget to thank the people who are usually overlooked. Each and every contribution is important and it is equally important to acknowledge their efforts. Appreciation can give the team members a satisfied feeling and motivate them to keep up the good work and engage with the same spirit in their next projects.

Your ultimate aim as a manager is to build synergy in your team. Synergy is the interaction of multiple elements in a system to produce an effect different from or greater than the sum of their individual effects. The 12 steps we saw can help you develop synergy in your team and achieve spectacular results in your endeavours.

Million Dollar Questions

Now that you are aware of the team's evolution, the team development model and the team building process, you need to know where you have to improve to achieve the *perfect* team. The following set of questions will help you evaluate your leadership and management skills and build a synergic team. Go through the checklist given below and find out the areas you have to work to *take charge of your team*.

1. Have you clearly conveyed your expectations from the team?

2. Do your team members understand the purpose of the team?

3. Has the team constructed a vision, mission and a plan for themselves?

4. Do your team members understand the importance of achieving the goal?

5. Are the team members excited about the goal?

6. Does the team have a complete road map?

7. Have you clearly defined the roles for all your team members?

8. Do they understand the relevance of their contribution?

9. Do your team members value their contribution in the bigger scheme of things?

10. Do they know how their contribution is going to enhance their career?

11. Are you providing enough resources to your team?

12. Have you provided your team with a timeline to keep the process in check?

13. Is the team aligned with the organisation's long-term strategy?

14. Have they made backup plans?

15. Are they aware of the strategic options available to them?

16. Is the team challenged and motivated to accomplish the given task?

17. Are your team members confident of themselves?

18. Are the team members confident about other team members?

19. Does the team have enough power to take decisions?

20. Do the members understand their responsibilities when it comes to decision-making?

21. Do the members understand the hierarchy of the organisation?

22. Do they understand their accountability?

23. Do they understand the code of conduct?

24. Do the team members understand each other's responsibilities, powers and limitations?

25. Is the group working towards a common goal?

26. Do the team members communicate effectively with themselves and with you?

27. Is there an established feedback mechanism?

28. Do the members find it easy to share their ideas with each other?

29. Are conflicts handled in a civilised manner?

30. Are your team members open to change?

31. Do they take risks or play safe?

32. Are they aware of the rewards associated with creative thinking?

33. Is your team aware of training mechanisms available to them?

34. Are the team members considerate and happy about each other's success?

35. Do your team members coordinate well with other teams?

36. Do the team members learn from their mistakes?

37. How well do they respond to criticism?

Answer the above questions to understand your team in a better way. Keep coming back to this list to make sure that you are on the right track. This checklist will provide you the real picture and remind you of the areas that you need to focus more.

Chapter Rewind

- Do not forget that you are the captain of the ship. You need to be in command so that your voyage reaches its destination in time.

- Team synergy helps foster creativity and innovation.

- Team spirit acts as an additional player on your side, which is often the difference between winning and losing.

- Great leaders are keen observers. Become a good observer.

- Leardership is earned. Walk your talk.

- You have to be tactful in your approach and react according to the development phase of your teams.

- Provide your team members with adequate feedback and let them know when their suggestions are implemented.

- Do not forget to thank people who are usually overlooked.

"It's not enough to be busy, so are the ants. The question is what are we busy about?"

-Henry David Thoreau

CHAPTER 3

TEAM DYNAMICS

The Goose Story

The Goose community set to fly from Canada to the south of United States, like they do every fall. The entire neighbourhood had taken off but Mr. and Mrs. Goose were busy preparing their seven little geese for the journey. Mrs. Goose was ready with the daughters, but Mr. Goose and the four sons were late as usual. After a lot of scampering around and last minute checks, the family finally took off.

It took a bit of effort to rise above the civilisation but once they were in the blue skies, it was familiar territory for them. The two big brothers very busy teasing their three sisters. Dreamer Goose, the youngest son, was lost in his thoughts while the Grumpy Goose was grumpy as always. Mr. Goose led the flight as they formed a V. They always flew in this formation, as it was aerodynamically optimal. Each member in the alignment provided additional lift and reduced air resistance for the goose flying behind it. The family discovered that when they flew in this formation they covered the distance quickly, with less effort.

After some time had elapsed, Mr. Goose was considerably tired so he shifted to the back where the air resistance was the least and Mrs. Goose assumed the leadership. This rotation is common among geese, when they have to cover long distances. The kids were constantly honking during the flight, teasing, laughing and motivating.

Grumpy moved out of the formation, as he was grumpy about not being given enough food. As soon as he dropped out, he realised that it required immense amount of effort to travel alone. He came back to resume the advantage of the lifting power that was the result of flying in V formation. The Goose family continued honking and enjoying their swift journey.

As they were nearing their destination, little Dreamer fell ill. He dropped out of the formation and the two eldest brothers escorted him, as the family moved towards their abode. The brothers nursed Dreamer and eventually caught up with their family. The Goose family was reunited. They reached their destination and spent a great time in the warm habitat.

This story is an epitome of teamwork. Every fall, the geese fly in v-formation to ease their effort in the long journey. They never lose the formation, as individual flying requires greater effort than team flying. They keep communicating amongst themselves to motivate each other. They change leadership so that one goose does not feel all the pressure. When one goose falls weak, others lend their support and ensure that he is taken care of. If geese can do it, then as humans we ought to do it.

The Beehive

Team and work are two separate words. But they assume great power when they are clubbed together to form 'teamwork'. So much so that they have been studied extensively to understand the importance of teamwork. The worker bees work in union diligently to build the beehive under the leadership of the queenbee.

Being part of a team gives its members a sense of belonging. When teammates come together and believe in teamwork, they look forward coming to work. They feel positive and that positivity is reflected in their work as well. Organisations harness this positive energy to keep their employees motivated and charged. You as a leader and a manger need to make sure that your team believes in teamwork. There are certain parameters that will allow you to monitor your team to determine whether it functions as a team or is individualistic in nature.

- **Sharing**

Does your team believe in sharing? Sharing can mean sharing of information, thoughts, feelings and goals. Communication and sharing transforms a group into a team and brings the team closer. There is a difference between a group and a team. A group is a bunch of individuals but teams are an entity of their own. There is no scope for individual identity in a team. A sharing audit will allow you to determine if your team works together or just sits together.

> A group is a bunch of individuals but teams are an entity of their own.

- **Helping**

Strong teams do not shy away from asking help or giving help. Well-built teams have members with distinct qualities and they constantly look out for each other and move towards their goal. Check if your team has members who push each other forward or pull them down.

- **Inculcating The 3 A's and C's**

Your entire teamwork module can be based on the three A's and C's. The three A's stand for Appreciating, Accepting and Acknowledging. Your team members need to appreciate, accept, and acknowledge each other's efforts. This feeling should not be superficial; it should be genuine.

The three C's stand for Criticising, Complaining and Condemning. Ensure that your team members engage in these activities only if it is going to add value to the team. These activities should not be performed to bring the other person down.

- **Valuing**

Team members need to value themselves as well as each other. It is your job to make the members feel valued. The teamwork equation will depend on how your team members value each other. Value generation is an integral aspect of team building. Analyse if each member of your team knows the contribution and hence value of all the team members.

- **Feedback**

Sound feedback mechanism is a culmination of the above-mentioned points. It cannot be generated unless your team believes in sharing, helping, valuing each other and positively engaging in executing the 3 A's and C's. Feedback makes sure that your team progresses fluently towards its goal. As a manager, you need to ensure that your team gives and receives feedback without any fear or bias.

- **Augmenting Team's Efforts**

Strong teams harness each other's strengths and develop success strategies. They indulge in convergent thinking and build on each other's ideas. Team members listen to each other's point of view and build on it. Check if your team members work synergistically towards the common goal.

- **Engaging in Calculated Risks**

Teams that believe in teamwork do not fear taking risks. They bank on each other's abilities and back the team to emerge victorious in trying circumstances. Risk-taking ability is often the deciding factor between good teams and great teams. Evaluate whether your team is prepared or hesitant to take calculated risks.

Teamwork negates ego and fosters a friendly environment. It lifts up the team's morale and that is essential for a team's success. Team dynamics plays a crucial role in determining whether a team will be able to work as a unit. Check your team's teamwork quotient from the points we just saw.

Right Shoe Right Fit

Maintaining team dynamics is not about just recruiting the best players. It is about choosing the right players depending upon the situation. Just as you cannot wear a left-foot shoe on your right foot no matter how appealing the shoe is, a placing a person at the wrong position will not work no matter how strong his/her résumé seems to be. Talent management is an ability that every manager must possess to take charge of the team.

Every position demands certain qualities; the right person must have the requisite skills and knowledge to deliver the requirements of the position. You cannot hire a mechanical engineer to perform the tasks of a computer engineer. You have to choose an individual equipped with the skills for the particular position.

The right player is someone who is entering in your desired profile at the right time in his/her career. You do not want to be stuck with a person who is on the wrong side of the fifties for a job that is suited for teenagers. Nor do you want a novice to lead a department.

The right player must be able to do the right things. He/she should be productive in the task. You want the player to spend bulk of his time doing what he/she is hired to do. You do not want your team members to focus on mundane stuff and overlook their job profile.

> The right player should possess high emotional as well as intelligence quotient.

The right way means that the team member is showcasing his/her talent in an ethical manner. The behaviour of the team member must be in synchronisation with the team's values and beliefs. For example, a new recruit must not make fake promises and resort to unethical ways to achieve his/her goal.

The right player is someone who is in the right position, at the right time, doing the right things in the right way. To ensure smooth team dynamics, you must recruit the right team member. Teams generally look at knowledge, skills and ability to assess the employability but they fail to look at the behavioural aspect of the candidate. The right player should possess high emotional as well as intelligence quotient.

Finding the Right Shoe

Suppose you have to choose the right player to fit your team. The team can be a new one, existing one or specially assembled for a particular task. How do you find the right players?

Your team players must be chosen in alignment with the team's goals. The timeline also needs to be considered. If the deadline is short, then there is no scope for training, which means that you need to hire seasoned members.

Your team needs to have a blend of experience as well as youth. Always think long-term while building a team. The experienced members can hold the fort, and the young players can bring in enthusiasm and energy.

Identify and make a note of attributes like aggressiveness, passiveness, compassion, dedication, etc. Such attributes can help you build a formidable mix while constructing a team. This is vital to maintain the right team dynamics, as members possessing different attributes can challenge and complement each other.

Check how passionate the members are about achieving the goal. If a member is passionate about the task, he/she is self-motivated. You do not need to exert extra effort to go out of your zone and motivate him/her. If a member is passionate about the task, he/she will perform the task with full concentration and determination. For instance, a person with a creative background will be the right choice for a team that has to create a storyboard for an advertisement.

You need to choose appropriately skilled people for the job. If you select an over-skilled person to perform a regular job, he is going to feel bored and unchallenged. If you recruit an under-skilled person to perform the task, then he is going to crumble under pressure. For instance, a branch manager will not feel motivated to cold call prospective clients. Similarly, a junior developer cannot perform as a Project Manager. Hence, you need to choose the person with adequate skill set in your team.

Make sure that the individuals challenge each other's point of view in a healthy manner. Productivity will multiply when members build on each other's base. You also need to keep an eye on certain personalities who overshadow others.

Do not add or subtract team members unnecessarily. Adding extra members will reduce productivity, as not everyone will contribute to their potential. Subtracting members will increase unnecessary pressure.

A team should include members who possess strong interpersonal skills. A team is an interdependent entity, thus a candidate must have strong interpersonal skills along with the above-mentioned attributes to be a part of the team.

Six Cats, One Mouse and a Storage Room

"I saw that son of a mouse hide behind the old engine. It is all yours, oh mighty saviour of the realm!" said Green Cat continuing his sycophancy.
"We are in for a treat then, my fellow cats," said Black Cat with a wicked smile as he lunged forward.

"No offense leader, but that is what you've been saying for the past two times," Brown Cat snapped at Black Cat.

"Why don't we throw gas bombs in there and smoke the little mouse out!" suggested Pink Cat.

"Didn't I tell you to shut your 'garbage hole' two minutes ago? It stinks whenever you say something," said Purple Cat rejecting Pink Cat's suggestion with disdain.

"What do you have to say Yellow Cat?" asked the leader in a condescending manner.

"You know what, I have had enough of your leadership. This dimwit hasn't spoken for a year and you want his opinion on this. I don't trust you anymore; I am going in. Those who want to eat can come with me," said Brown Cat.

Brown Cat jumped at the huge box behind which the mouse was seeking refuge. Purple Cat joined him in the pursuit, but failed to locate the mouse. They were busy searching the storage room when they heard some noise near the window.

Yellow Cat finally spoke up, "Look, the mouse is jumping out of the window!"

The six cats looked at the mouse that was at the threshold of the window. "You are never going to learn, are you? You waste a lot of time thinking than doing. I wrote an entire book, while you were busy hatching a plan. Take this, you need it." The mouse threw a book at the six cats and jumped out of the window. The book was titled 'How to Improve Team Dynamics' – By Mr. Mouse.

The above story is a perfect example of bad team dynamics. Some member is busy acting as a sycophant, the leader has no plans, and another member does not trust the leader anymore. No one gives valuable suggestions, suggestions get ridiculed, there is no mutual respect, opinions are not valued so members are afraid to speak up, there is a rift in the team and finally the task stays unaccomplished.

When Everything Goes Wrong

Bad team dynamics often takes shape when there is a glitch in team selection. It also culminates when there is weak leadership. Other dominant member takes over and there is confusion regarding the leader. Teams start to focus on all the wrong things. Members do not voice their opinion and agree with whatever the leader has to say.

Few members block the thought process of the team by intervening when it is not necessary. The aggressor disagrees with everyone, the negative member criticises everyone's ideas, the withdrawer does not participate in the discussion, the boastful member blows his own trumpet and the joker makes inappropriate jokes. This is a disastrous situation for a team!

Making Things Right

It is extremely valuable to know your team and the stage at which your team is functioning. You need to address the issues as soon as you notice them. Tackle problems quickly by giving prompt feedback. Define roles and responsibilities and break down barriers. Pay attention to details and focus on communication. Good dynamics can motivate the team to achieve great heights. It keeps the atmosphere light and builds camaraderie between team members.

Leader-Member Exchange Theory

- **Circle of Trust**

It is natural for a manger to trust his team members. But it is also natural that the manger is more open and trustworthy with a few members. If you have ever managed a team, you might find this situation a lot familiar. You do not treat every team member the same way. You have built a relationship with certain team members over a period, and thus share a bond with them. You trust them and they trust you, they work hard and you reward them accordingly. As they reciprocate positively, you end up sending challenging projects to them.

Apart from the trusted members, there are a few others with whom you don't connect. You do not think highly of them and assign them with mundane and everyday responsibilities. They do not have huge aspirations regarding their careers and are often overlooked when it comes to promotions.

You consciously and subconsciously slot people into a Circle of Trust. You involve certain people in your Circle of Trust, while keep a few people away from it deliberately. However, as a manger you need to understand the core reason for this sort of classification. Is the classification because of their traits or because of your subconscious conditioning? Managers are human too and often, humans tend to be judgemental about others quickly and irrationally.

> Managers often tend to be judgemental about others quickly and irrationally.

- **Formation of the Circle**

The formation of the Circle of Trust starts right when the team member joins the team. Managers take time to understand the new member's performance. The skills and abilities are scrutinised and strengths and weaknesses are established. Managers assign tasks to new members and expect them to be loyal and sincere in their approach.

If the members reciprocate and meet the demands of their manager, they land a place in the Circle of Trust. The manager believes in the players who are a part of the circle. The manager takes efforts to look into their career growth and assigns challenging and interesting assignments that help them to enhance their career in the organisation. Members who possess similar traits to the manager are often a part of the Circle of Trust.

Members who do not live up to the expectations of the manager are not allowed into the circle. The manager views them as incompetent and unmotivated. As a result, they are neglected and are deprived of training and development, growth opportunities and interesting assignments.

The members who are a part of the circle are perceived as rising stars and continue to work hard to stay in the prestigious clan. The left-out members are de-motivated and are on the look out to change their team or the department so that they can make a fresh start.

Widen the Circle

While a Circle of Trust may be humanely impossible to avoid, you need to ensure that all your resources are utilised efficiently. By segregating your team, you are missing out on valuable resources. It is imperative to widen your Circle of Trust to include all your team members in it.

For that, you will have to analyse your team and make a note of the members who are out of your circle. Find out the reasons they are considered outsiders. Is it because their lack of performance or is it because of your perception that you have abandoned them? Once you have found out the reason, you have to work towards establishing a relationship. If they lack in performance, you need to motivate them. If you have sidelined them because of your restricted perception, you need to engage in one-on-one conversation with them and understand them better.

The leader-member exchange theory warns you about your unfair behaviour towards a certain section of your team. By introspecting, you will be able to connect with your team and help the team perform to their potential.

Chapter Rewind

- Don't just stay busy; stay productive.

- Develop a game plan. Not having a game plan is like wanting to construct a tower, without a foundation.

- Team and work are two separate words. But they assume great power when they are clubbed together to form 'teamwork'.

- The teamwork equation will depend on how your team members value each other.

- Teams that believe in teamwork do not fear taking risk.

- Good dynamic can motivate the team to achieve great heights.

- Productivity will multiply when members build on each other's base.

- It is vital to maintain the right team dynamics, as members possessing different attributes can challenge and complement each other.

"Someone's sitting in the shade today because someone planted a tree a long time ago."

-Warren Buffett

CHAPTER 4

TEAM PERSONALITIES

Forwards and Backs

The CEO of a multinational company asked a consultant to deliver a speech highlighting the importance of teamwork and various team personalities. The conference's theme was based on sales and marketing, so the consultant structured his speech around the two warring departments of the organisation.

There was visible friction between the sales and marketing team. The marketing staff accused the sales team of not following the organisation's strategy and the sales team blamed the marketing department for not working diligently. The consultant thought he could address the issue by using a rugby analogy. He elaborated how in a rugby team the forwards and backs play in unison and work closely to achieve the team's goal.

The consultant concluded his speech by saying, "Your organisation also functions like a rugby team. In a game of rugby, the forwards spot the opportunities and pass the ball to the backs to score the tries. In an organisational set up, the forwards or the marketing team spots opportunities and creates a base for the backs, or the sales team to seal the deal and accomplish targets. The forwards and the backs just like the marketing and the sales team may be good at doing their job. But the team only wins, when they play together." The rugby analogy was a hit; the audience cheered and the CEO was happy with the response.

The conference broke for lunch and the consultant bumped into a member of the sales team. He asked him for his opinion on the speech. The salesperson acknowledged the analogy and accepted that the sales team was the backs and the marketing team was the forwards. He also appreciated the thought that when forwards and backs work together, the team wins. Just before he turned to leave, he said to the consultant. "You know what, you are right, we win when our forwards and backs perform together, but I still think the forwards are a bunch of idiots."

Even though the consultant made a great effort by giving the rugby example to explain his point of view, it did not achieve the expected results. This is because teams have individuals with diverse personalities. A manager or a leader needs to handle these personalities delicately to maintain the right balance between them. It is important to understand the personality of your team members and address their issues accordingly.

Five Fingers of A Hand

The nature of your team dynamics is dependent on the personalities of your team members. Every individual has a peculiar perception. This diversity in a team helps in analysing a situation from various vantage points. Each of our fingers on a hand is of different physiological dimensions. The different shapes enable the fingers to perform different functions for holding, gripping, manoeuvring, and so on.

> Diversity in a team helps in analysing a situation from various vantage points.

As a team leader, you have to evaluate the diverse personalities in your team and spot their unique talent or skills. Understanding various personality traits can help you assess the strengths and weaknesses of your team, which in turn will help you empathise with your team members and work more efficiently.

Some personalities contribute to the goal while some may create a disturbance. You need to review and manage all types of team personalities professionally to achieve success.

Let's delve into various personalities you may encounter in a team and ways to handle them. For better understanding. The personalities have been classified as 'Contributor' and 'Difficult.'

Contributor Personalities

Contributors are personalities who help achieve your team goal. These personalities contribute immensely in converting your team into a high performance team.

- **Silent Contributor:** People belonging to this personality type do not boast of their performance. They get the job done without any hassle. If your team has a silent contributor, make sure you motivate him/her to speak up, as it will keep the team's communication channel flowing.

- **Devil's Advocate:** This type of personality keeps your tasks in check. Such a person likes to challenge the status quo. The Devil's Advocate brings new ideas to the table. He/she engages in positive conflict, which provides the team with an optimum solution.

> Contributiors are personalities who help achieve your team goal.

- **Facilitator:** Facilitators bring order in the team. They believe in controlled situations. They do not allow the situation to get out of hand. They help the team to channelize their energy and work towards the common cause. They get things done without any chaos.

- **Leaders:** Some people are born to lead. They have a natural flair to inspire people and lead them. Leaders are good at delegating and motivating people to accomplish the task. They take charge to empower others in order to achieve success.

- **Followers:** These are the people who do the bulk of the work. They do not have any problem following instructions and do so to perfection. They work hard on the assigned tasks and ensure its timely completion.

Check your team to ensure there is a balance of these five contributor personality types in the team. They will prove extremely beneficial for you in the long run. These personalities will hold your team together even when it multiplies. Such members are highly motivated and performance-driven individuals. Allow them to function according to their plans. Play a supervisory role while dealing with such members, as they know what they are doing and do not need much interference in their work.

Difficult Personalities

Teams also have difficult personalities. It is important to manage them to ensure that your team functions to its potential. We can further classified the difficult personalities under four categories: Aggressive, Deceptive, Passive and Destructive.

Aggressive Personalities

Aggressive people have an issue controlling their anger. They exhibit aggressive behaviour and are unable to resolve conflicts. They charge and vent out their frustration on others. Here are personality types that fall under aggressive:

- **Perfectionists:** They strive for perfection and become hostile when things are not perfect. They are fastidious critics of both their work and others' work. They set unrealistic standards and make the workplace uncomfortable for others. Such personalities need to develop emotional intelligence. You must communicate with them to make them understand the ramifications of their obsessive behaviour.

- **Dictator:** This type of person likes to be in control of the situation. A dictator is demanding and condescending. They are always angry and create a nuisance for passive team members who crumble under pressure. You have to be tactful when you come across such dictators in your team. Since others cannot regulate such people, they need to practice self-regulation. Your role is to encourage them to align their attitude.

- **Hostile:** Hostile people create havoc in the organisational setting. They have anger issues, which lead to abusive confrontations. They are constantly argumentative and thrive on chaos. They cause turbulent situations because they view it as an opportunity to be in the spotlight. Like other aggressive personalities, they need to practice self-regulation and need to keep a tab on their impulse and disruptive emotions. They need to think before they act.

To handle such holistic individuals, you as the team leader should be a person whom they can trust in problematic situations. You must have a calming influence. This can be achieved through constant one-to-one communications.

- **Attackers:** Attackers have no control over their anger. They need to vent out their frustration to be normal. They are on the lookout on whom they can take it out. Slight things upset them, and when they are upset, they need someone who can listen to their pain. Generally, these people get hyper when they face changes. They should be encouraged to be open to new ideas.

- **Egotists:** An egoist thinks he/she is superior to everyone. Such people think of themselves as experts and criticize everything. They do not like to take orders and behave in an arrogant manner. They point out problems and like to criticize to feel important. They need to inculcate empathy. They need to understand how other person feels when he is criticised for no fault. If any of your team members is an egotist, he will obey you or follow your instructions only when he respects you. Thus, you should earn the respect of such a person to manage him/her efficiently.

- **Bully:** Bullies like to intimidate others. It is their way of gaining popularity and power. They humiliate others to project false superiority. They consider anyone who is likeable and attractive, a threat. They only look at things from their point of view. You need to be assertive with them and tell them that their actions do not contribute to the reward that they think are eligible to receive.

- **Criticiser:** Such people often complain about everything that is new. They resist change and like to point it out. They constantly provide negative feedback. Such people respond to all requests with a no. You have to be diplomatic in your approach and help them polish their social skills and practice conflict management.

Deceptive Personalities

They are not aggressive in nature and do not confront any situation directly. They attack behind the back and disrupt the functioning of an organisation. They remain aloof and plot the downfall.

- **Snipers:** They are silent when it comes to voicing their opinion on a public forum but are very aggressive while speaking behind someone's back. They use humour and sarcasm to humiliate others. Snipers hide behind the scene and plot to pull others down. They make it difficult to trace their involvement in the plot. Snipers need to be in check of their emotions and develop emotional awareness. You need to help them realize the negative effects of their deceptive nature.

- **'Yes' People:** People who say yes to everything and everyone fall under this category. They have a problem saying no to others and often end up with too much to handle. They do not take a stand and agree with everyone on everything. 'Yes' people are a huge hindrance when it comes to decision-making. Help them realize that it is their inability to say no that puts them in a tight spot and that it is all right to say no to people. Such people have to be self-aware and assertive while dealing with others.

> 'Yes' people are a huge hindrance when it comes to decision-making.

- **Bootlickers:** They believe that the shortest way to success is to agree and flatter the boss. They do not believe in voicing their opinion. Show them that honesty is the best policy and that they need to foster integrity if they want to succeed in the long run. They need to maintain certain standards for themselves.

- **Escapists:** Such type of people are least bothered about their work. They give excuses and shy away from doing their work. They waste their time and indulge in a lot of personal work during office hours. Escapists are often unresponsive and hence, it is difficult to understand them. Be assertive with them and tell them that they need to sort out their priorities in life.

- **Rumourmongers:** There are always rumourmongers in a team who spread rumours to generate strong responses or attention from others. Rumourmongers feel important when they hear people speak about the news they shared with them. They make it difficult to trace the source of the rumour. Help such people in your team and motivate them to work with others and stay focused on their goal. They need to concentrate on productive issues and refrain from such demeaning acts.

Passive Personalities

Passive personalities are negative by nature. They project themselves as weak and reject any solution provided to them. They do not cope with change and need to be constantly motivated.

- **Martyrs:** They feel they sacrifice everything for their organisation and yet their efforts go unappreciated. The do not have a social life and often work overtime. They put in long working hours and constantly complain about peers, managers and everything else. Show them that it is important to be not only an efficient and productive player, but also be a smart worker to receive recognition in an organisation.

- **Passive-Aggressive:** This type of people are aggressive but in an indirect manner. They express their emotions by beating around the bush and by avoiding confrontations. They often resort to hostile jokes, express sullenness, act stubborn, and procrastinate. They feel jealous and threatened by others. They also display intentional inefficiency. You can help such passive-aggressive team members by helping them improve their self-esteem.

- **Crybabies:** People belonging to this personality type behave like children when things do not go according to their wish. They withdraw and create a fuss till their demands are met. They project themselves to be powerless and consider everything to be negative. They need to realise that such behaviour is not going to work in the long run. Only self-regulation can redeem them.

- **Self-castigators:** Self-confidence and self-esteem are alien terms for such type of people. They drown in self-doubt even when their performance is up to the mark. This person takes the blame for everything that goes wrong and depreciates one's self-worth time and again. The only way to revive such self-castigators types of people is to help them develop a positive outlook to life.

- **Worriers:** As the name suggests, they worry a lot. They create scenarios in their head and keep worrying about them. They are deeply hurt by negative comments and often complain about being stressed. As a manger, you need to motivate such people and tell them to concentrate on things that are in their control rather than worrying about something that is not.

- **Resisters:** They are allergic to change. Resisters are comfortable only in certain situations and are affected by anything that challenges their comfort zone. They will do everything in their capacity to avoid change if they find it too threatening. You need to cultivate a sense of achievement in such resisters. Help them view change as an opportunity rather than a threat.

> Help them view change as an opportunity rather than a threat.

- **Lone wolf:** A lone wolf always works in isolation. Such people do not like to function in a team. If forced to work in a team setting, they go in a shell and refuse to contribute. You need to show the significance of social skills and encourage them to work in a team.

- **Neglecters:** People belonging to this category neglect anything that according to them is not under their job profile. In an organisational setting, we may have to perform some tasks that are out of our job description for the wellbeing of our team. Neglecters refuse to perform such activities and often consider it a way to get back at someone or sometimes the organisation itself. Explain the importance of teamwork and create a team synergy to motivate them to pursue collective goals.

Destructive Personalities

People falling under this category can be a threat to themselves as well as the team. Their behaviour is unpredictable and hazardous to team harmony. They can disrupt the working of an organisation by their uncontrolled outbursts. Their social life is in turmoil, and due to it, their professional life also takes a hit.

Help such individuals maintain healthy work-life balance. They should be trained to control their emotions. Ensure that your team members communicate with them both formally and informally and try to uplift them. Make them understand their self-worth and cultivate optimism to help them lead a positive life.

Each personality is different and needs to be treated accordingly. Sometimes, you may come across people who have a combination of personalities. Human behaviour is complex and needs to be dealt with cautiously. You need to work with your team members to help them orient their attitude and follow good conduct. They need to realise that their behaviour is detrimental to their future in the organisation, it is only then that they will take efforts to change. Motivate them and make them realise their follies so that they can work on them for a better future.

Chapter Rewind

- A manager or a leader needs to handle various personalities delicately to maintain the right balance between them.

- The nature of your team dynamics is dependent on the personalities of your team members.

- Understanding various personality traits can help you assess the strength and weaknesses of your team, which in turn will help you empathise with your team members and work more efficiently.

- Some personalities contribute to the goal while some may create a disturbance. You need to review and manage all types of team personalities professionally to achieve success.

- Play a supervisory role while dealing with team members falling under contributor personalities, as they know what they are doing and do not need much interference in their work.

- You need to work with your team members to help them orient their attitude and follow good conduct.

"There are no constraints on the human mind, no walls around the human spirit, no barriers to our progress except those we ourselves erect"

-Ronald Reagan

CHAPTER 5

COMMUNICATION

Jacob and John

This is the story of two managers, named Jacob and John. Jacob was task oriented; all he cared about was performance. He had a reserved personality and kept to himself. Having set stringent production and quality standards, Jacob had high expectations from his team members. He was known for firing people who failed to meet his expectations. Team members feared his presence. He gave short feedbacks, only when necessary. It was difficult to get a word of praise from him. Employees considered themselves to be praised if they were not criticized.

John was friendly and mingled well with his team members. He believed in recognition of achievement and appreciation. Team members felt relaxed in his presence, as he was a bit on the lenient side when it came to meeting production and quality standards. John understood that it was difficult for team members to give their best every time; as a result, he rarely fired anyone. He did not believe in direct confrontation and expected his team members to understand his cues, when it came to performance reviews. John never made the team members feel uneasy, but due to his leniency, there were a lot of management-related issues and minor crises.

Suppose, you had to choose Jacob or John as your manager, whom would you choose to work for? Which of the two would you choose as your role model?

At the outset, John may seem more popular and easier to work with. However, we have to consider the bigger picture here. Jacob may be intimidating, but he tells his team members the reality upfront and provides clear-cut roles and expectations. Team members know exactly where they stand. They understand that they have to perform or perish; there is no middle ground.

There are no weak links in your team when you are working under Jacob. As a team member, you will only have to take care of your tasks and not shoulder the burden of other unproductive members. Under Jacob, you will be a part of a productive team and learn a lot. There will be no scope for flattery and you will *earn* your praise.

John settles for mediocre work in pursuit of being kind. John might be productive in the short run, but Jacob will succeed in the end. Jacob will build a high performance team for the future. However, he also needs to learn a few things from John to take charge of his team. Many aspiring managers and leaders choose to play John. They choose to be lenient in order to avoid being assertive or unpleasant. They prefer to be in the good books of their team members and compensate on quality in the process. Managers like John settle for a situation in which both the parties are content and do not demand much from each other.

If choose to work for and work as Jacob and incorporate empathy and appreciation qualities from John, you would be respected and admired by your peers and team members alike.

Mirroring Ants

If you have ever observed a line of Ants you would have seen that sore tires, an ant, usually at the end of the line, would touch another ants head. The second ant would then turn in another direction while the first ant continues to do the same down the line what the ants are actually doing is communication. Yes ants communicate through their antennas. This communication helps them work collectively when there is a perceived danger or proximity of food.

Communication is vital if you want your team to achieve the goal. You need to clearly communicate the goal and the individual roles, and give them prompt feedback to ensure that your team stays on track.

Your performance as a manager is directly dependent on your communication skills. This relation holds true for every organisation. You have to communicate with your team members as well as your superiors to manage your daily chores. If you closely analyse the profile of a team leader or a manager, you will notice the importance of communication.

A manager spends most of his time communicating. He is either receiving or sending information to his team members and to other departments. Managers persuade, explain, ask or give information on a constant basis. You won't achieve your purpose if you are not able to communicate effectively.

Communicating with your friends and family is different from communicating with your team members. Just because you communicate splendidly in your personal life does not guarantee that you will be a successful communicator in your professional life. Professional communication has its own share of challenges. You have to be formal in your tone but informal in your approach while dealing with your team members.

> You have to be formal in your tone but informal in your approach while dealing with your team members.

It is a known fact that great managers are great communicators. Most of the managers are good at communication with certain type of people and in certain situations. However, they have to learn to communicate effectively under all circumstances and with everyone.

Effective communication depends what you say and how you say it. Different people perceive information differently. A manager should communicate in a way that can be understood by people from different walks of life. People tend to listen carefully to their superiors but fail to do so when it comes to dealing with subordinates. You should avoid such a bias and remove all kinds of barriers while communicating.

Communication does not end with delegation; it needs to be followed by sound feedback. Effective communication and constructive feedback will ensure that your team stays aligned with your goal.

7 Open Secrets

You are bound to communicate with a lot of departments in your role as a manger. You will have to communicate internally as well as externally. Your success will invariably depend on how well you communicate. Here are seven open secrets of effective communication will equip you to be a master of the art.

Be Positive

- Keep the environment positive. Positivity fosters productivity. Be positive in giving feedback and appreciating your team members. Avoid gossiping and speaking negatively. Lead by example.

- Create a bond with your team members. Your team members are not machines; they have emotions. Maintaining a positive emotional connect will build a strong relationship between you and your team members.

- Remember that you can communicate even when you are not talking. Positive non-verbal communication is as important as verbal communication. Your eye contact, body language and tone of voice also create a great impact on how others receive the information.

- Create an open communication environment. Encourage your team members to communicate with you. Have an open-door policy. When you are busy and you cannot meet someone, decline meeting him/her kindly and reschedule an appointment. Be open with your team members and maintain a friendly relationship with them.

Be Conscientious

- Convey a message only if you are hundred percent sure about its authenticity. You do not want to lose your credibility by communicating something that is not true. Your team members should not question the information coming from you. There should be trust between both the parties.

- It is not necessary to answer all questions but it is necessary to answer questions correctly. It is better to avoid giving an answer when you don't know the answer rather than answering it wrongly. You can always get back to the team member afterwards with the correct answer.

- Do not use jargons. Keep your communication simple. You should communicate in a manner that can be easily understood by a supervisor as well as an executive. When you convey your message in a simple manner there are less chances of it being misinterpreted.

- Explain your decisions to your team. Ensure that they understand why a particular decision was made. Explain how it is going to affect or not affect them. Keeping them in the loop of things would make them feel a part of the decision.

> Acting on impulse is not a good way of resolving a problem.

- Do not let emotions control you, be in control of your emotions. Do not react to situations instinctively. Take time to analyse and then respond. Do not communicate when you are angry. Let the emotions settle down; convey your thoughts after some time. Acting on impulse is not a good way of resolving a problem.

- Accept your mistakes and correct them. Do not hesitate to apologise to your team members if you have faltered somewhere. Do not make promises that you cannot keep.

- Respect others privacy. Do not discuss personal issues of a team member with anyone else. Deal with sensitive information tactfully. Respond to your members' queries. Be precise in your communication. Keep your information short and to the point.

Listen

- People underestimate the power of listening. Listening is as important as speaking. You have to listen actively so that you can understand and respond aptly. Listen without getting deviated.

- Respect the person with whom you are conversing. Keep your gadgets away while engaging in a conversation. Use paraphrasing to show that you have understood.

- You can also show you are listening through attentive body language.

- Do not judge other people by the manner in which they speak.

Stay Connected

- Stay in touch with your superiors and convey instructions clearly to your team effectively. Conduct meetings regularly so that your team members are aware and up-to-date with the recent happenings.

- Review your team's goals periodically and ensure that everyone is aware about them. Evaluate your team members' work and communicate with them about the areas they have excelled and area where they need to put in more effort. Encourage them to attend seminars and undergo training and development sessions to hone their skills.

Give & Receive Feedback

- Help your members improve their performance by giving them concrete feedback. Encourage them to give suggestions and feedback. This healthy give-and-take will keep the team productive.

- Ask experts in your team for their suggestions in relevant situations. Not everyone might be able to come forward and explain his/her views. Encourage such members to share. Proper feedback will increase productivity and enhance the bond between the manager and the team members.

Be Direct, Honest, Upfront

- Be direct in your approach. Do not beat around the bush while conveying your message, especially if you are conveying bad news. Being direct reduces tension. Choose the right time and location to talk.

- The golden rule in management is to appreciate in front of everyone and criticize in isolation. Anticipate most likely questions and be prepared with the answers. Be honest and upfront in your answers.

- Allow your team members to absorb the information you have provided to them. Give them some time to analyse the situation and come up with a response.

Handle Conflict

- Conflicts are a natural occurrence in a group setting. The first step to resolve a conflict is to acknowledge it and then to solve it by discussing openly. Conflicts can increase absenteeism and provoke arguments. It is important to stay neutral while dealing with conflicts. Make sure you hear every party before jumping to conclusions.

- Communication is the only way to resolve conflicts. Conflicts can give rise to positive conclusions if dealt with professionally. Handle conflicts as soon as they arise. Take preventive measures before the problem escalates into an uncontrollable situation. Speak to the members in reckoning and calm them down.

You will be able to take charge of your team by practicing the seven secrets of effective communication. Be receptive as well as vocal. It is better to think before you speak than think after you have spoken. Maintain a rapport with your team by communicating with them regularly.

> It is better to think before you speak than think after you have spoken.

Huddle up

Team meetings are part of a healthy routine and are a productive way for bringing your team up-to-date. You can monitor individual as well as team efforts with the help of regular meetings. It facilitates efficient and quick decision-making.

Personal interaction is a must in today's dynamic scenario. Strong work relationships can be built when team members are in touch with each other. Regular meetings will strengthen the bond between team members and keep a track of the work. Ideas can be exchanged and the team can be constantly updated about recent developments.

Team members can be intimated about any change in strategy and ways to achieve the renewed goal through team meetings. Team meetings are also a good platform to acknowledge the work done by your team. Praising team members for their efforts in a public setting will boost their morale and motivate them to aspire for more.

Team meetings provide the much-needed personal touch in today's technologically advanced world. Crucial matters can be discussed and innovative ideas can be generated through brainstorming. Team meetings are important for the success of an organisation. Team meetings help assess the situation and plan your strategy accordingly.

Points to Remember

Meetings ensure that teams function at a personal as well as interpersonal level. Just like every other aspect of an organisation, meetings also need to be managed.

- Meetings should have a clear agenda. You also have to clarify who needs to attend the meetings and what should they come prepared with.

- Although creative and innovative team members might attend meetings, the result is not always productive. This can be avoided if you manage your meetings in a professional manner.

- Decide if the meeting is really necessary, manage team dynamics and give everyone a fair chance to express themselves.

- Do not let anyone dominate the meeting, summarise a person's conversation, if he is going a bit overboard, and allow the reticent member to contribute.

- Whether you are a team leader or a team member, you should approach team meetings as a student. You should keep your ego at home and attend meetings to learn.

Come prepared for the meeting and do not deviate from the topic. Many times people drift away from the agenda and view team meetings a platform to settle scores with each other. Try to avoid these things and build over each other's opinions to generate a productive scenario.

A few members may be a bit reluctant to admit that have not followed certain points discussed. You as a facilitator need to make sure that everyone has followed and make a note of summarising everyone's contributions.

Listen attentively and contribute intelligently when you are part of a meeting. People tend to agree with everything that is being discussed. Meetings are not a one-way transmission of knowledge, there has to be a conversation, a healthy discussion.

The success of a team meeting depends upon how it is being managed. Team members may consider team meetings a waste of time, or lose interest in working together. Use the meeting tips to take charge of your meetings and conduct a productive session.

> The success of a team meeting depends upon how it is being managed.

The Call Centre Research

A manager at a bank's call centre was baffled by the inconsistent performance of some of his teams. All his teams were similar while a few excelled beyond expectations, the others faltered in their pursuit. He analysed the performance metrics but could not find out a particular reason for the gaps.

A research team was called in to identify what was causing the difference in performance among the teams. They conducted studies across various industries on teams working in post-op hospital wards, front desk teams in banks, back office teams, and call centre teams. Teams with varied performance were analysed. The skills possessed by call centre employees were easily identifiable. They were clear and easy to monitor. The parameters on which their performance was evaluated were number of issues resolved, customer satisfaction and average handling time. The team came up with two major conclusions.

The research team found out that the one factor that was not accounted in the performance evaluation metrics was communication. The study suggested that communication was a major aspect when it came to successful teams. The other, more astounding conclusion was that communication was not driven by content, but the manner in which it was carried.

During the research, members of the selected teams had been given electronic badges that stored information regarding their communication. The tone in which they spoke, the clarity with which they spoke, their pitch etc., was noted by the device. All these factors were considered to analyse the communication pattern of the teams.

Sound communication played a critical role in fostering team spirit. The results of the research were consistent across successful teams belonging to diverse industries. Teams that were productive displayed team synergy and engagement outside formal settings.

From the study, it was clear that communication builds teams, and teams perform at an optimum level, when team members communicate with each other formally as well as informally.

The manager of the bank's call centre, taking cue from the research, scheduled the coffee break of team members at the same time. This common break opened an avenue for communication and the team began to socialise informally. Team members connected with each other, away from their workstations. This gave rise to increased employee satisfaction along with an increase in the productivity level. Communication played a pivotal role in enhancing productivity and building an effective team.

A Space Odyssey

Suppose your team is sent into space for exploring the moon, but your spaceship crash-lands on the moon. The rough landing causes considerable damage to the spaceship and ruins the equipment. There are only 15 items available at your disposal.

Your mother ship is waiting for your team on the lighted surface of the moon that is 200 miles away from your current destination. Now, your task is to rank the below mentioned items in the order of their importance for your journey to the mother ship.

Mark the most important item for your survival as 1, 2, and so on. Ask your team members to first rank individually. Then, work together and gather the team rankings. Make a note of the error points as well to ascertain your proximity to the original rankings.

Item	Your Ranking	Error Points	NASA's Ranking	Team Ranking	Error Points
Box of matches					
Food concentrate					
50 feet of nylon rope					
Parachute silk					
Solar-powered portable heating unit					
Two .45 calibre pistols					
One case of dehydrated milk					
Three 100-pound tanks of oxygen					
Stellar map of the moon's constellation					
Self-inflating raft					
Magnetic compass					

Item	Your Ranking	Error Points	NASA's Ranking	Team Ranking	Error Points
Five gallons of water					
Signal flares					
First-aid kit injection needles					
Solar-powered FM Receiver-Transmitter					

After you have both individual and team rankings, compare it with what NASA has to say and find out if you would have reached the spaceship or not.

Item	Actual Ranking by NASA
Box of matches	15
Food concentrate	4
50 feet of nylon rope	6
Parachute silk	8
Solar-powered portable heating unit	13
Two .45 calibre pistols	11
One case of dehydrated milk	12
Three 100-pound tanks of oxygen	1
Stellar map of the moon's constellation	3
Self-inflating raft	9
Magnetic compass	14
Five gallons of water	2
Signal flares	10
First-aid kit injection needles	7
Solar-powered FM Receiver-Transmitter	5

This Space Odyssey is not just interesting, but also reveals surprising results. Use this model to test whether individuals are in synchronisation with the team. When team comes together, communicates effectively and works in unison, anything can be achieved.

Chapter Rewind

- Communication is vital if you want your team to achieve the goal.

- Lead by example.

- Create a bond with your team members. Your team members are not machines; they have emotions.

- Convey a message only if you are hundred percent sure about its authenticity.

- Accept your mistakes and correct them.

- The golden rule in management is to appreciate in front of everyone and criticize in isolation.

"The best executive is one who has sense enough to pick good people to do what he wants done, and self-restraint enough to keep from meddling with them while they do it."

-Theodore Roosevelt

CHAPTER 6

DELEGATION AND PERFORMANCE

The New Driver

Jack was considerably nervous. It was his first day as a bus driver at the medical facility. His manager assigned him the duty of transporting a dozen mentally challenged patients from one branch to another. Jack obliged and took the bus to the assigned mental facility. He completed the necessary formalities and the twelve patients were seated in the bus. The journey commenced to the other facility that was about 250 miles away.

After driving for about an hour and a half, Jack stopped at a restaurant to take a break and refresh. As he returned, he was shocked to find all the twelve patients missing from the bus. He was devastated and feared the consequences of facing his manager. He thought for a while and drove the bus to the nearby bus stop. He quickly made up a story and said that his was the replacement for the regular bus. He waited till twelve passengers boarded the bus, and drove to the mental facility.

The people in the bus started panicking when they realized that the driver had taken them to a different destination. As he entered the gates of the mental facility, he cautioned the staff to be careful and alert, since the patients were deluded and violent. Even as the passengers protested, the staff at the mental facility sedated and incarcerated the twelve normal people instead of the twelve patients who escaped away. Jack, fearing consequence also fled.

The passengers brought in by Jack were kept in the mental facility for three days before their identities were confirmed. Neither Jack, not the twelve patients who went missing, could ever be found!

This is allegedly a true story that emphasises the perils of wrong delegation. Before delegating work to your team members, you need to be aware about the capabilities of the person. Intelligence quotient is alone not enough; emotional quotient also needs to be taken into consideration.

Diligent Delegation

Managers' job is to manage the work, not to perform all the work on their own. Teams exist because an individual cannot accomplish the volume of work required to be completed. When you have a team at your disposal, why do you want to do all the work by yourself? Assigning work to the right candidate is one of the important duties and responsibilities of a team leader.

You will end up with a lot of work and ultimately strain yourself if you refrain from delegating. All the unfinished tasks will pile up and cause unwanted stress. Nevertheless, you may feel that when you delegate work to others, they may not give hundred percent to it. You may not be sure whether others will perform the task with the same intensity with which you would have performed it. This dilemma can be solved with proper delegation. The right candidate will perform the task as demanded and relieve you of stress.

What, When and Whom

Before assigning a job to your team members, you need to decide what to delegate, when to delegate, and whom to delegate. The nature and timing of the job are crucial factors in deciding the right person. You cannot delegate a task to your team members if it is due in an hour. You will end up explaining and training the team member about it most of the time or end up compensating on the quality.

Before delegating, you must check the availability of a person worthy of the task. The team member should possess the relevant skills to successfully achieve the goal. Some team member may have more experience and expertise in preparing a video presentation than you do. In such case, you can delegate such a task to that person and create a window for approving or changing the content of the presentation before it is finalised.

The time factor needs to be considered while delegating a particular task. You should be able to provide the necessary training and make necessary corrections within the stipulated time.

You also need to take a call whether you want to delegate to one person or a team. If you delegate too much work to one person, he/she will get exhausted, but if you assign too less to a team, it will result in waste of resources. Make sure that the people to whom you delegate report to you to keep a track of the progress. If you delegate work to cross-functional teams, it gets difficult to monitor the work.

The commitment level of the staff needs to be considered before a job is assigned. You can even ask for suggestions from your team members regarding the delegation. There might be someone who may voluntarily take up the job.

> The commitment level of the staff needs to be considered before a job is assigned.

Behind the Scenes

Imagine the time when you came out of the cinema after watching an awe-inspiring movie. You felt thrilled. From the minute to the last, the movie engrossed you. There were no plot holes, no hiccups; the movie simply flowed. Do you think the execution was as smooth as the movie itself? That's hardly ever the case. Everyone looks at the 2-hour movie, but never the effort behind it. What happens behind the scenes is an example of efficient delegation process.

The delegation process should be crisp and clear. As a team leader, you must know what you have assigned to others and what you have to concentrate on. Team members should understand their role and responsibility to accomplish the assigned task.

- Be clear about the desired outcome of the task. Inform your team members about their contribution in the ultimate goal of the team. Be specific about the desired result.

- Explain the chain of command to the person you delegate to. She should know who is authorised to give her orders and whom she should report to. If the team member is not clear regarding the hierarchy, he will end up obeying orders from everyone, resulting in chaos.

- Ask if anyone is willing to volunteer to accept the job. Delegating the job to someone who is passionate about it will be beneficial for you as well as the person. Empower them to make decisions. This will save time in the long run.

- Although you are passing some of the responsibility of the task to your team members, you cannot pass the accountability to someone else. You are accountable for the task. Hence it is necessary to keep track of the progress.

- Assign the task to a person who is best suited to perform the task. Do not be biased while delegating.

- Provide the necessary training to the team member you have chosen for the task. Keep the communication channels open and closely monitor the activities of the team member. Provide all the resources that the person might need to achieve the task. Keep her motivated by reminding about the reward attached to the goal.

- Do not spoon-feed the candidate. Let her apply her mind and come up with creative solutions. She might find a way to solve the problem more quickly and efficiently.

- Once you have chosen the candidate or the team, shift the control. Let them control things their way. You should be concerned about the result. Trust and confidence will allow them freedom to perform to the best of their abilities.

- Review the progress periodically without interfering in the work. Make necessary changes along the way and keep communicating and motivating your team. Make sure you praise good work.

Delegation is a part of time management strategy. Proper delegation can result in a win-win situation for you and your team.

Say NO to Micromanagement

Once you assign a particular task to a team member and allot a deadline, do not constantly interfere in his/her work. If you keep checking the progress by sending emails and nagging continuously, then you are a micromanager. Micromanagers do not empower their employees; they criticize and frustrate team members. Managers and team leaders are often not aware about their micromanaging stints.

Micromanagers want to control their team members. They do not allow the team to function independently. You are a micromanager if you resist delegating work, constantly keep a watch on others projects, correct minute details, find mistakes in unfinished work and bar others from making decisions without being consulted.

> Micromanagement is Restrictive in nature. It does not allow the team members to grow.

Delegation fosters empowerment while micromanagement restricts it. It cripples the team member, as they are forced to depend on the team leader for everything. The manager spends lots of time and energy so that he can be in control. If an entire team is restricted and depends on the manager to proceed further, it is going to be counterproductive in the long run. Micromanagement is restrictive in nature. It does not allow the team members to grow. You should trust your team members and provide them with opportunities to grow.

Stanford Prison Experiment

The Stanford prison experiment depicts the extremes to which one can go when he/she is driven by power. Dr. Philip Zimbardo conducted an experiment on delegation and group dynamics in the year 1971 at Stanford University. A mock prison was set up at the university to study the effects of delegation of power. Twenty-four middle-class graduates were selected for the experiment. The mock prison was rigged with cameras to observe the inmates.

They were divided randomly as prisoners and guards. The guards had the liberty to work in shifts but the prisoners were not given any such luxuries. The guards were also given unrestricted power to maintain order in the prison.

The experiment revealed the dark side of human nature. It was observed that while essaying the role of guards, normal people became extremely aggressive and humiliated the prisoners for no fault. They became violent under the mask of anonymity. A few guards questioned the behaviour in the beginning but joined hands to traumatise the prisoners after succumbing to peer pressure. The guards violated human rights while punishing the prisoners even when the prisoners had not committed any crime to face such wrath. Their aggression escalated, as there was no accountability.

The experiment was supposed to last fourteen days but was terminated after only six days. The guards continued their inhuman acts forcing the prisoners to rebel against them, to which they retaliated with more aggression. The video footage was so disturbing and unethical that it couldn't be shared. The experiment revealed that it was so easy for those in an authoritative position to turn dark and resort to violent means.

Human beings behave differently and transform drastically when they are vested with power. The people who essayed the role of guards displayed no remorse for their inhuman acts after the experiment. They believed that they had behaved appropriately under the given circumstances.

Power has to be vested in the right hands; it has the capacity to corrupt even the strongest of individuals. As a team leader, you need delegate tasks to the right individual and empower the right candidates.

One Bad Apple

Workplace negativity demoralises team spirit. It creates a rift between team members and reduces productivity. Negativity germinates due to lack of confidence and control, and sometimes, due to unpleasant change or rumours. You have to be vigil, understand the source of negativity and eradicate it from the core. Here are a few pointers that will help you eradicate negativity from your team to enhance its performance:

> Negativity germinates due to lack of confidence and control, and sometimes, due to unpleasant change or rumours.

- Let team members contribute in making decisions that affect their job. Autocratic control by the manager can render the team powerless. They feel shackled and make plans to break free. Give them the freedom and flexibility to express themselves. Invite suggestions and accept them if they are fruitful.

- Changes in work hours, salary, overtime, leaves, etc., affect team members the most. Such issues are close to them and challenge their presence in the team. Unpleasant changes in these areas can trigger negative consequences. Be proactive and do not let negativity sink in.

- Do not be biased to team members, as it is one of the main causes for negativity in a team. You may have your personal favourite players but do not let it affect the team policies. You have to set a standard and stick to it. You cannot be partial towards a particular member. Be fair and consistent in your approach.

- Your team members are mature adults, treat them accordingly. Do not create unnecessary rules for everyone, when only a few members have defaulted.

- Guide your team whenever necessary. Reward your team members and make them feel a part of the team. Lead your team with a goal-oriented attitude.

This way, you can align your team to a positive state of mind and not let negativity hamper the performance.

Champion of Champions

High-performance teams constitute of individuals who are highly focused on their goals, and exceed expectations every time. The team members complement each other and are willing to sacrifice for the team's benefit. They contribute by providing creative solutions and overcome all barriers to accomplish the team's goals. Successful sports and business teams display the characteristics of high-performance teams:

- **Participative Leadership:** High-performance teams have leaders who practice participative leadership. They do not believe in autocratic leadership and consider the views of all the team members before reaching conclusions. This democratic leadership is instrumental in engaging the team members and reaching a consensus quickly.

- **Team Decision-making:** Decisions are made rationally as well as intuitively. Rational decisions are based on facts and statistics, while intuitive decisions are made on the feeling. The situation at hand usually guides the type of decision made. Ensure that decisions that directly affect the team are made after a discussion with all the members.

- **Effective Communication:** The team members are like a family. They share their feelings with each other. They communicate all the time and this communication does not allow conflicts and negativity to seep in.

- **Diversity:** High-performance teams project unity in diversity, which helps them look at situations from various vantage points. The different perspectives allow the team to think and act differently.

- **Trust:** Team members trust each other. This trust allows the team to venture into unfamiliar territory and emerge as winners. The team members are not afraid to take risks, as they know that the other members are there to back them in case of an adversity.

- **Constructive Conflict Resolution:** It is natural for team members to have diverse opinions. Sometimes, the situation might heat up and result in a conflict. High-performance teams handle conflicts in a professional and a transparent way.

- **Defined Goals:** High-performance teams have well-defined goals for individuals and for teams. Team members are committed to their goals and help each other to meet individual goals, so that the team goal can be met easily.

- **Optimistic:** The teams believe in a positive and transparent work environment.

High-performance teams are self-motivated and only need the right guidance to move successfully. The team members of high-performance teams are highly skilled and are able to interchange their roles.

> High-performance teams are self-motivated and only need the right guidance to move successfully.

Chapter Rewind

- All of us have only 24 hrs in a day. Prioritising will help you make the most of it.

- Teams exist because an individual cannot accomplish the volume of work required to be completed.

- The nature and deadline of the job are crucial factors in deciding the right person to do it.

- Human beings behave differently and transform drastically when they are vested with power.

- Power has to be vested in the right hands; it has the capacity to corrupt even the strongest of individuals.

- Ensure that decisions that directly affect the team are made after a discussion with all the members.

"Never, never, never, never give up."

-Winston Churchill

CHAPTER 7

MOTIVATION

"Realign the attitude of your team to transform it into a high-performance team."

Coffee Lessons

Sarah, a young girl of 17, was depressed. She found it difficult to cope with life's challenges. Her mother recognised the change in her daughter and approached her about the problem. Sarah shared her worries, and confessed that she was tired of facing one problem after another and wanted to run away from all this. Sarah's mother listened calmly and took her to the kitchen.

The mother filled three pots with water and heated them. When the water started boiling, she placed carrots, eggs and coffee beans in each of the three pots. She allowed the ingredients to boil. After twenty minutes, she removed them from the pots and placed them in a bowl.

Sarah's mother asked her to come close and touch the ingredients that were placed in the bowls. Sarah touched the carrot and noticed that it was soft. Next, she picked up an egg, broke its shell, and observed the hardboiled egg. Later, she sipped the coffee and enjoyed its rich aroma and the taste.

Sarah's mother explained to her that the three objects had faced the same difficulty: boiling water, but they had reacted differently to it. The hard and strong carrot turned soft and weak. The fragile raw egg hardened. But the coffee beans were a class apart; they managed to change the boiling water!

Each and every one of us faces problems, but what matters is our reaction to it. Do we react like the carrot, which seems strong and hard at the outset but becomes weak and soft after facing an adversity? Do we react like an egg, which becomes void of any emotions after facing a setback? Or do we react like the coffee beans, which change the circumstances that cause pain. Do we accept the challenge and change the circumstances in our favour?

Your team members should be like the coffee beans. They should be self-motivated to achieve tasks by overcoming challenges. Like the coffee beans, motivated team members can change the circumstances that cause pain. They question the status quo and tilt the result in their favour. You will be able to achieve great heights with a motivated team.

> Motivated team members can change the circumstances that cause pain.

Good Tyres and Punctured Tyres

Motivation is the idea that fuels our actions. It is essential for each and every member of a team to stay motivated. It is not possible to drive a car with a punctured tyre. All the four tyres need to be in good shape. Similarly, the team members must be motivated to support each other to achieve the team goal.

We perform a task because we are motivated to act. Self-motivation may have a personal or professional reason, but there is always a reason for what we do. Sometimes, we are not even aware of the reasons; they may be stored in our subconscious mind. We do things because we are ought to derive something out of it or we fear the consequences of not doing a particular thing. Most of our decisions are governed by this principle. We make decisions based on the consequences: positive or negative.

Team motivation is based on needs. These needs have a wide range; they can be related to security, growth, recognition, etc. But motivation is what drives the team to meet the needs, achieve rewards and avoid negative consequences, just as tyres in good shape are required for a smooth journey towards the destination.

Motivation Source

Here are some sources of motivation you can explore to recharge your teams:

- **Purpose**

The team needs to have a clear mission to concentrate on. The purpose is what drives them to accomplish the task. Short-term tasks can be achieved even if the team members don't connect with the purpose or the goal. But if your team has to succeed in the long run, your team members need to be given a purpose that will add value to them. Their individual purpose also needs to be aligned with the team purpose.

- **Challenge**

Challenges motivate your team to outperform your achievements. History suggests that humans are driven by challenges and look forward to them. We are hardwired with two responses when faced with a challenge: fight or flight. Set such challenges that your team becomes motivated to overcome it, but not so high, that it gets dejected and quits. The fear of failure also acts as a motivator, along with the quest of reaching new heights.

- **Team spirit**

Team spirit can motivate your team members to work hard for each other. Members who share a great camaraderie look out for each other and complement each other. Whether you like or dislike a person is fundamentally based on whether you understand that person or not. Disputes may arise because of this.

Once your team shares and understands each other in a better manner, your team members are bound to develop a liking for each other. This camaraderie results in a motivation to work in unison, put in additional effort to make up for other team members' weaknesses and build on the strengths.

- **Responsibility**

Team members become more cautious and aware of the environment when they are given responsibility. Make them accountable for their actions. This motivates them to perform better. There is a sense of ownership and authority attached with responsibility and that is what motivates a person to give their hundred percent.

- **Growth**

Employees strive for personal as well as professional growth. Growth is associated with self-esteem and self-worth. If you set a task that is going to reward them with such growth opportunities, your team members are going to be highly motivated to achieve it.

- **Leadership**

History has taught us the value of great leadership. Leaders are instrumental in stimulating motivation in team members. You can lead by example and inspire your team to perform exceptionally.

However, leaders can only inspire up to a certain level, it cannot be a continuous process. Strong teams constitute of self-motivated individuals. If you want your team to be successful in the long run, your members should be self-motivated. Initially, leadership can act as a catalyst to conjure motivation but at the end, it is up to the individual to get motivated and be inspired from within.

> You can lead by example and inspire your team to perform exceptionally.

Initially, your team may need direction and motivation, but as it grows, your team members need to become self-motivated.

Simple Ways to Recharge Your Team

Managers tend to concentrate too much on the big picture and fail to look at the simple day-to-day activities. By following simple ways, you can motivate your team members to enhance their performance:

- Make your team members feel a part of the group. Involve them in the decisions that affect them.

- Acknowledge their presence by exchanging pleasantries. Even a good morning has the power to stimulate your team members and increase their confidence.

- Take interest in your team members' work. Ensure that they know that you value their efforts.

- Stay in touch with your team formally as well as informally. Formal interactions will definitely take place during meetings but interact informally by demonstrating your concern for your team members. Ask them about their recent vacations and bond with them by discussing their favourite movies or books.

- Offer team members opportunities to display their skills by delegating challenging and interesting work. Team members do not like monotony.

- Involve your team members while representing your team in meetings or seminars. This will give them a sense of belonging.

- Showcase your trust on your team by empowering them. Praise and reward them on their outstanding performance. For major achievements, arrange felicitation ceremonies to credit your team members. Settle complaints promptly.

- Listen to the ideas put forth by your team members. Incorporate their suggestions wherever suitable. Do not jump to conclusions; understand the team member's point of view. Do not slam or shun the idea. Explain why it is not foolproof.

Theory X and Theory Y

In the chapter related to team personalities, we saw distinct personalities in a team and their approach towards a team's goals. Theory X and Theory Y club the nature of different individuals in two categories. The first category consists of people who like their work and take great pride in performing their tasks. People belonging to the second category view their job as a burden and work merely for financial benefits.

The two personality types are distinct and need to be motivated differently. Theory X deals with people who are least interested in their jobs and work only for monetary rewards. Theory X warrants for an authoritative style of management. People belonging to this category need to be controlled and told what to do. They need constant supervision, and perform to their potential only when they are threatened. Management cannot afford to empower such type of people, as they are only motivated by financial benefits and job security.

Team members belonging in the second category need to be managed using Theory Y principles. Theory Y speaks for a decentralised management. It deals with people who are self-motivated. They are happy with their work and relish responsibility. They need to be motivated by giving responsibility and authority. Managers need to follow participative management while dealing with people belonging to this category. You can motivate such team members by empowering them and giving the freedom to do their task in their approach.

As a team leader and a manager, you need to identify which team member belongs to which category and motivate him accordingly. Theory X principles cannot be applied to a person falling under theory Y category. Imagine assigning responsibility to a person, who dislikes his job; it would lead to a disastrous situation. Use the two theories smartly to motivate your team.

Being the Linchpin of Your Team

You may face a situation in your life as a leader, where you may have to stand by your team when the chips are down. In such situations, support your team even if they have performed slightly less than expectations. Back your team and explain to the senior management why the team failed to live up to the expectations. If there was a fault from the management's side, communicate the same diplomatically yet assertively. If a

Your support to the team when everything seems to go downhill will reinstable your team's faith in you and act as a motivator to live up to your expectations.

particular team member failed to perform to potential, you must assume responsibility and face the management's wrath to defend that team member.

But before standing up for your team, you should analyse the situation. You should not compromise on the team's values to safeguard someone who has used unethical ways. Do not distinguish while standing up for people. Make sure that they do not repeat their mistake, once you have taken the blame for their actions.

Sometimes, you will have to defend your team from the senior management's allegations. Make sure you have your facts right before arguing with the senior management. It is important to stay united in a time of crisis. Your support to the team when everything seems to go downhill will reinstate your team's faith in you and act as a motivator to live up to your expectations.

Mobile Management

You have to be open in your approach towards your team. A manager who sits in a closed cabin is often oblivious to the trials and tribulations of his team. By practicing mobile management, your team will view you as a human and not just a manager. This will help you bond with the team and maintain a friendly yet professional work atmosphere. You have to communicate to your team that they can contact you for help any time. If you create a barrier between yourself and your team, you are creating a rift in the team at the outset. The manager and the team need to be a unit.

> By practicing mobile management, your team will view you as a human and not just a manager.

By practicing mobile management, you will become proactive and solve problems before they even arise. Your team will view you as approachable and come to you with their problems before they escalate into something that may be detrimental to the organisation's success. By mingling with the team, you will be able to gain their trust; they will offer it to you willingly. By meeting your team members and understanding their work ethic, you will get to know their work approach and process in a better way. This will eventually contribute in drafting strategies for the long run. Being in touch with your team builds accountability and increases productivity.

While practicing mobile management, ensure that you are not interfering in your team member's private space. Ensure that you are not being biased in your approach to a particular member. Answer queries and do not be judgemental about any one. Team members might not be used to watching you mingling around with them. It is natural for them to be a bit nervous. Keep your eyes and ears open. When your team feels that you care, they will not want to let you down.

Chapter Rewind

- It's not about how many times you fall down; it's a question of how many times you get up.

- We make decisions based on the consequences: positive or negative.

- The fear of failure also acts as a motivator, along with the quest of reaching new heights.

- Initially, leadership can act as a catalyst to conjure motivation but at the end, it is up to the individual to get motivated and be inspired from within.

- The manager and the team need to be a unit.

- Strong teams constitute of self-motivated individuals.

Offer team members opportunities to display their skills by delegating challenging and interesting work.

CHAPTER 8

TEAM EMPOWERMENT

The Cookie Dilemma

Robert was a hardcore foodie, and loved sweets the most. His friends called him a "cookie maniac", because he could never resist a cookie once his eyes fell on it. His sweet tooth had eventually led to some health and weight problems, and he was bound to keep a check on his diet.

One morning, while he was skimming through the newspaper, an advertisement grabbed his attention. A new bakery had opened hardly 30 minutes away from where Robert stayed. What mostly interested him was that the bakery claimed to focus on healthy cookies that were low on fats and sugar content.

Robert visited the bakery that same day after work. Delicious sweets and cookies were all around him. It took a lot of guts to control his sweet-munching instincts. At one end, the tasty chocolate chip cookies were inviting him, while at the other end, his doctor's advice ringed in his ears, "Don't yield to your temptations". Robert reluctantly turned his attention to the oatmeal cookie section.

One of the store vendors noticed this dilemma in Robert's eyes and went to him. He pointed towards a set of delectable looking chocolate chip cookies. Robert reluctantly shook his head and enquired about the price of the oatmeal cookies.

"These chocolate chip cookies are really yummy", the vendor said, "Why don't you try them?"

"No, thanks. How much do the oatmeal cookies cost?" Robert asked hesitatingly.

The vendor noticed the twinge of doubt in Robert's refusal, and asked Robert again if he wanted the chocolate chip ones. Robert refused and finally paid for his oatmeal cookies. As he walked out of the store, he was proud of not giving in to his temptation, but also loathed the fact that he couldn't devour the chocolate chip cookies. On reaching home, Robert opened the package and found two chocolate chip cookies! He realised that the vendor had secretly slipped them in. This pleasantly surprised Robert.

On his next visit, Robert asked the vendor about this. The vendor politely replied, "Our bakery encourages us to take decisions on our own as long as we adhere to its values." Robert was amazed by the management principles and of course, the extra chocolate chip cookies and became a regular customer.

More Power for Empowerment

One of the key approaches of successful managers is the empowerment of their team members. They know that a team works and achieves its targets because of the individual and the collective inputs of its members. At the end of the day, the team effort is what matters.

What is empowerment then? It is nothing but involvement of the team members – the setting up of a milieu that encourages people to take calculated risks and make their own decisions for the greater good of the team. Empowerment is not a task, nor a tool of management; it is a management philosophy about how people can be encouraged to give their best.

> Empowerment is not a task, not a tool of management; it is a management philosophy about how people can be encouraged to give their best.

When you trust your team members' abilities, it reciprocates. They would in turn trust your vision for the team, and give their best towards achieving it.

All For One, One for All

Engaging your team members by encouraging them to make important decisions harnesses more benefits than are obvious. When you involve your team in all facets of the work at hand, it increases their commitment and keeps them motivated. It builds an environment where people have a sense of ownership and therefore choose to contribute. Empowered members believe that they sculpt their own success through their efforts and hard work, thereby benefitting the entire team and the organisation.

Let's take a closer look at some of the positive impacts of team empowerment:

1. Improved Quality of Work

When people realise a sense of purpose, they tend to produce better results. Team members feel more connected with their workplace when they feel that they are playing an active role in the team's and the organisation's proceedings. This encourages them to deliver high-quality work. Empowered people take their job more as a responsibility than a burden. This keeps them from being demotivated in times of failure and being complacent with success.

2. Job Satisfaction

If team members are granted the power to identify problems and provide solutions on their own, they become highly motivated, because then they take pride in their jobs. This in turn gives way to increased ownership of responsibility and greater job satisfaction. On the other hand, if people are not given the freedom to take independent decisions, in addition to losing a sense of responsibility, they get bored with their jobs, thereby decreasing productivity.

3. Coaction

Treating people as a vital component of the organisation boosts their self-confidence in positively contributing to the vision. This in turn encourages a collaborative space of work, where information and ideas flow freely, promoting teamwork and coaction in an honest and open manner. The team members are more actively involved in the achievement of the team's and the organisation's goals.

4. Increased Productivity and Reduced Costs

Empowered people work diligently to meet challenges and strive to give their best at every level. They feel energised to achieve the goals and do it the right way. This therefore, increases the individual as well as the overall productivity, providing better performance results for the organisation.

Empowerment of the team members also reduces costs as the turnover decreases. With employees being more satisfied with their work, their sense of loyalty towards the organisation increases. It also enhances efficiency due to increased accountability.

The rationale of giving members the freedom to take independent decisions and calculated risks to solve a problem, makes them more motivated and committed. Because of this, the team as well as the organisation steadily moves towards growth and development. People accept and adapt to the changes that come across and strive to give an optimal performance.

How much Empowerment is Empowerment?

We saw the advantages of empowering your team members and making them more accountable for their work. However, you may face certain challenges in implementing team empowerment effectively.

One of the problems that arise while implementing empowerment is that people infer it as a tool of management rather than a philosophy. People think of empowerment as something that needs to be bestowed on someone by someone. Many times, it so happens that the team members wait for the managers to empower them, while consequently, the manager asks why they aren't proactive and engage themselves in the task. This leads to a general dissatisfaction and disappointment in the team, hampering performance.

Rather, think of empowerment as something that comes from within. It is a process in which individuals enable themselves to control work and decision-making in a self-reliant manner. However, no matter how much your team members are empowered, it will add up to nothing if the work environment isn't appropriate, i.e., if it doesn't encourage people to stay motivated. A work place that follows a strictly hierarchical structure discourages active participation of the employees. A flexible working environment, on the other hand, drives self-confidence in people and keeps them motivated.

Again, an overly flexible work atmosphere might be detrimental. All said and done, at the end of the day, the manager is accountable for any catastrophic results of a poor decision. Therefore, it takes a mature manager to decide how much to yield and how much to retain, and what levels of involvement should be created in the team.

> Decide how much to yield and how much to retain, and what levels of involvement should be created in the team.

Tannenbaum and Schmidt's model of delegation and team development gives a detailed insight into the overall impact of team empowerment. It describes a continuum, that shows the relationship between the level of freedom a manager chooses to give to the team, and the level of authority used by the manager. Given below are the levels of the continuum.

1. Decide and Announce

The manager solely takes the decision, without consulting the team. He/she reviews the situation, considers the priorities, and weighs the options, to decide upon a solution. He/she then directly announces the decision to the team, and the team plays no active part in the decision-making process. The team sees this as a purely task-based decision.

2. Decide and Sell

The manager takes the decision, as in the above level, without consulting with the team on any matter. However, in this level, the manager "sells" the decision to the team, i.e. he explains to the members the rationale behind the decision. In doing so, the team sees the manager as one who recognises the team's importance and has some concern.

3.   Present Decision and Invite Questions

In this level, the manager presents the decision that he/she has already taken to the team, along with some background ideas that led to the decision. The team is given the freedom to discuss and raise queries, enabling the team to understand and accept the decision more easily than in the other two levels.

4.   Suggest Decision and Discuss

A provisional solution is decided upon by the manager, which he/she puts forward for discussion by the team. The manager collects relevant pointers and ideas from the discussion and implements them to arrive at an optimal solution. This raises the team's spirits, as the team members feel that they have more or less an active role to play in the organisation's growth and development.

5.   Get Suggestions and Decide

The situation is presented to the team, along with some insights and options. The team is encouraged to suggest some relevant ideas and a possible course of action. The manager then decides according to the suggestions given by the team. This boosts up the spirits of the team members, as it requires a relatively higher level of team involvement.

6.   Delegate Responsibility to Decide

The situation is presented, the parameters are defined, and the team is asked to decide upon the course of action. In this level, the manager effectively delegates the responsibility of decision-making to the team; however, the result is in the manager's control. This level is of course more motivational than the previous ones, but it also requires a highly mature team to take the appropriate decisions.

7.   Yield Decision-making

In this level, the team decides as the manager does in level 1. It takes into account the situation, considers the options, identifies the priorities and parameters, and then decides on its own, without any intervention from the manager. This level is the most motivational, but also the most precarious, requiring a highly mature team to handle really tough decisions.

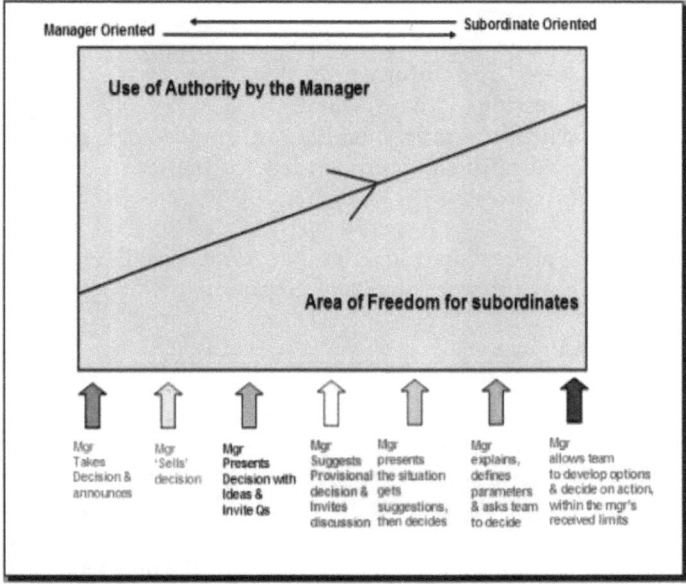

Tannenbaum and Schmidt's Model of Delegation

Ultimately, it is in your hands to decide what level of involvement to implement in your team. You can use the pointers below to increase the level of involvement in your team:

- Your skills and experience

- Your team members' skills and experience

- The knowledge of external factors that affect the decision-making

- Individuals' self-efficacy

- The team members' degree of commitment to the organisation

- The level of freedom you have for implementing high levels of involvement

Credo of Empowerment

An empowering manager trusts the team to do the right thing. He/she doesn't fetter the team members by limiting the tools and information required. Creating a work

> An empowering manager trusts the team to do the right thing.

environment where the team members are empowered, productive, contributing, and satisfied, does wonders for the team's success and the organisation's growth.

However, there are certain principles that you must follow to manage your team in a way that involves and empowers them. They are:

1.   People Power

You should accept the fact that people are more important than management systems and tools. The way a management system functions or the management tools perform depends on how the people in the team/organisation react to them. In other words, people bring in with them differences and changes that make a system conducive. Projects come and go, while people stay. They are the ones who develop, design, and finish projects. This is why maintaining the physical and emotional wellbeing of people becomes necessary.

How you regard your team members shines through your words and actions. Your body language, facial expressions, and your interaction with team members in general, express what you think about them. A manager's simple smile combined with polite behaviour goes a long way to retain people's motivation.

2.   High Involvement

In today's fast-paced world, high involvement is inevitable. The more the employees are in control of their work functions, the higher the productivity of the team and the organisation. The reason for this is that structured management systems have a great negative impact on the overall performance, as they deter collaboration and cohesion. When your team members assume responsibility of their tasks and are equally accountable, they feel that they are in control of the situation, and that their efforts have a considerable effect on the organisation's success.

To ensure maximum involvement, share the team vision and goals with your team members. This would help them feel that they are a part of something bigger than themselves and their individual jobs. Ensure that your team has well-defined goals, mission and strategic plans and make them easily accessible to your team members.

3. Working Together Works

As we have seen in the earlier chapters, teamwork has three significant benefits:

- Greater efficiency
- Synergism
- Better resource utilisation

Empowered teams tend to put the team's goals and vision in the foreground, and work accordingly. However, there are two vital components of empowered teams:

- Full expression of individual abilities
- Necessity of interdependence

Teamwork is essential for the team to be empowered, because only when team members work in synergy and be accountable for their work, the team goal can be achieved.

Encourage teamwork by maintaining transparency and motivating collective efforts. Point out how the team's job as a whole affects the organisation's wellbeing and reward good efforts.

4. The Learning Curve

Professional and personal growth goes hand-in-hand in empowered teams. Being a dynamic process, empowerment enables individuals to continuously set goals for

> Professional and personal growth goes hand-in-hand in empowered teams.

themselves and achieve them. This fosters a growth in their career. Similarly, when there is high involvement, people-oriented skills become necessary, which in turn enables personal growth. Moreover, people start enjoying their jobs because of the need for continual personal development.

By providing a work environment where your team members are actively involved, you can ensure that they grow personally as well as professionally.

5. Encouraging Onus of 'I'

When members of a team are aware of their individual responsibility and their responsibility towards the team, and when they are accountable for their actions, the team tends to be more cohesive. A predisposed mindset for complete responsibility and accountability towards the task not only increases productivity, but also enhances job satisfaction.

Without these two factors, empowerment ends up being a vague concept. This is because unless people are responsible towards the task at hand and accountable for their actions, there can never be any sense of ownership. The more difficult of the two is for people to accept and face the consequences of their actions. Accountability is probably what limits maximum involvement.

6. Promoting Positive 'Selfie' Attitude

Empowering requires people to be motivated and committed towards achieving the common goals. Most of the team members, if not all, should be able to perform their jobs with the least amount of oversight and management. Difficulties arise when people lack the self-determination during tough times. People need to be on their heels to face challenges and to adapt to change.

As has already been stated, empowerment comes from within. Promote self-motivation among your team members. Because a person's will to meet and possibly exceed the job expectations is what motivates and consequently empowers him/her.

7.   Delegate Authority, Not Just Work

Delegation is an essential principle of empowerment. You should be ready to delegate critical responsibilities to the team members. For that, you must trust your team to do the right thing.

A great way of building up an empowered and productive team is to delegate crucial tasks to your team members. Delegating just routine work might hamper the performance of your team. You should also delegate critical tasks, like important meetings, decision-making, and projects that peers and customers will notice. This will boost your team members' spirits to hone their skills. It will also lighten some of your responsibilities, so that you can concentrate on contribution to the team.

8.   Responsible Delegation

The act of delegation itself is not empowerment. The process of delegating responsibilities within clearly defined constraints to the right person is what enables empowerment. It depends on the individual's ability to aptly carry the responsibility entrusted to him and fulfil it. If you pass decision-making to your team members without taking into consideration whether they have the right skills, you cannot achieve the results you expect. At the end of the day, the problem needs to be solved, not complicated.

Delegating responsibility just for the sake of it will only result in demotivation. Therefore, ensure that you choose the right candidate to do a particular task.

9.   No to Restrictive Hierarchy

Traditional hierarchical structures hamper teamwork and collaborative efforts. Hierarchy and superiority/inferiority complexes come in the way of performance and hinder efficiency. To produce effective results, people must be able to trust and be frank with each other. Only then, can there be a free flow of ideas and information.

A hierarchical structure might sometimes lead to negative conflicts within the team, which is greatly unwarranted for. A flexible participative structure, on the other hand, breeds positive conflicts and a collaborative work environment. It paves the way for a workplace where coactions are welcome.

10. Commitment to Empowerment

Empowerment is impossible without a clear commitment from the manager's side. Manager must communicate the necessity and the desirability for empowerment and bind it with the organisation's core values.

For empowerment to take hold, you must practice what you preach. Live the empowerment vision and implement the core values. Lead by example.

Empowering the team members is one of the key practices that you must put into use, in order to maintain a healthy and effective working environment. Agreed that there is a lot of risk involved in assigning crucial decision-making tasks to the team members, but risks must be taken in order to extract the best.

> Risk must be taken in order to extract the best.

Chapter Rewind

- Empowered people take their job more as a responsibility than a burden.

- Empowered people work diligently to meet challenges and strive to give their best at every level.

- An empowering manager trusts the team to do the right thing.

- You should accepts the fact that people are more important than management system and tools.

- The process of delegating responsibilities within clearly defined constraints to the right person is what enables empowerment.

- To produce effective results, people must be able to trust and be frank with each other.

CHAPTER 9

CONFLICT RESOLUTION

"The reality today is that we are all interdependent and have to co-exist on this small planet. Therefore, the only sensible and intelligent way of resolving differences and clashes of interests, whether between individuals or nations, is through dialogue."

-The Dalai Lama

The Bane of Negativity

John was the manager of a great team, but one of its members, Paul had a particularly bad attitude. Before John had become the manager of the team, he had been a part of it along with Paul. Paul was quite senior to John in age. He was always negative, arrogant, and did not work in unison with the team most of the times. He would pass negative comments in a boisterous manner, which affected the team's overall performance. Knowing Paul's attitude, John decided to talk to him about this when he became the team manager. Paul seemed to show a change, but after a few days, went back to his usual self.

The team members were used to this Paul's negative attitude and went about their jobs, without paying much attention to him. However, problem arose when Paul had a verbal argument with one of his colleagues, Herbert. It was loud and incriminating, and disturbed everyone on the floor, including members from other teams. Jason intervened and asked both Paul and Herbert to meet him.

Jason talked to them separately, so as not to embarrass any one of them. He gave a verbal warning to Herbert, but a written warning to Paul, stating he was liable for termination if any such thing happened again.

This scared Paul and from that point on, he had no more attitude issues. His personality and character remained the same, but he restrained himself from passing negative and arrogant comments.

If Jason had chosen not to intervene, he would have created a rift in his team, which would only have resulted in decreased productivity. Conflicts are inevitable in a workplace. But if you ignore them or avoid them instead of handling them, you are only paving way for negativity and poor team synergy.

Conflict: A Definition

Before looking at the ways to handle conflicts, let's first define what we refer to as 'conflicts' in a team or an organisation. Conflict can be:

1. A serious disagreement or argument, typically a protracted one

2. A state of mind in which an individual experiences a clash of opposing needs

3. A serious incompatibility between two or more opinions, principles, or interests

Conflict in the Team

Conflicts arise due to diversity of team dynamics – people with differing backgrounds, culture, ideas, and attitudes that come together in an effort to accomplish a common goal. Conflict is a negative aspect that hampers the team's performance.

However, it is not always so. There can also be circumstances where conflicts can have positive effects. Sometimes, conflicts can become necessary to prevent complacency in a team and the dangerous effects of groupthink.

Tussles Team

Conflicts in a team can be of two types – positive and negative.

Positive Conflict

Conflicts are always difficult, but not all conflicts are always dysfunctional. They may also lead to growth and change. Some level of conflict is actually desirable. No one likes pain, but if you look at it this way, pain actually shows you how to react to it. If you accidentally put your leg on a nail and don't feel the pain, it is very dangerous. Unless you feel the nail pinching, you won't remove your leg from it.

When conflict arises, it is an alarm that there is something wrong happening – something that needs to be mended. Positive conflicts arise when a team is committed towards achieving the goal, because it would mean that, every individual is trying to come up with the best solution. Positive conflict in fact promotes challenge and increases the effort to resolve the issue. Without positive conflicts, an organisation will fail to adapt to change and hence will stagnate. Positive conflict especially prevents groupthink, and fosters effective decision-making.

Groupthink

Groupthink is a phenomenon that occurs in a team when its members, in their desire to maintain conformity, decide upon an incorrect or deviant solution. In their attempts to avoid conflict, the members reach a consensual decision without critically evaluating it.

This might prove quite harmful for the team and the organisation. To prevent a minor setback, one should not walk towards a dangerous situation. It would be similar to saving a person from heat by locking him/her in an ice chamber.

So, why does groupthink occur? It occurs because of the following reasons:

1. **Group cohesiveness** - Becomes more important than individual freedom of expression.

2.   **Structural faults** like lack of proper leadership, lack of norms requiring methodological procedures, homogeneity of members' social background and identity, etc. lead to groupthink.

3.   **Situational characteristics** like moral dilemmas, peer pressure, recent failures, etc. discourage the team members and give rise to groupthink.

Groupthink at outset may seem to have some benefits. In case of a large team, groupthink may enable faster decisions and efficient tasks. However, these come at the cost of suppression of creative thought and adaptability, which is a far bigger problem.

Positive conflict is highly effective in team discussions. In case of a conflict, the team will look for more information to resolve it. Since disagreements would be voiced, the team would conduct a more thorough investigation of the matter. When the team would finally reach a decision, it would be based on additional information that the team would never have come across, had the conflict not arisen. Therefore, positive conflicts suppress groupthink and encourage free flow of information, thoughts, and ideas.

By curbing groupthink, positive conflict brings in a sense of ownership, involvement, and enthusiasm from all group members, thereby encouraging application of creative thought processes and innovative ideas. When each team member is allowed to voice his/her own opinions and perspective, a more collaborative and active work environment is fostered. Moreover, when there is a positive conflict, individuals take active part in the decision-making process, and therefore have higher levels of satisfaction with their team.

> Positive conflict brings in a sense of ownership, involvement, and enthusiasm from all group members.

Negative Conflict

In heterogeneous teams, negative conflicts can arise due to the mere presence of diverse individuals with differing backgrounds, ideas, and agendas. Unlike positive conflicts, negative conflicts are better avoided. You must swiftly address and resolve them when they occur. Negative conflicts may dangerously impact the team morale and commitment, hampering productivity. It may be disastrous to such an extent that the team may ultimately be terminated. Negative conflicts can lead to consequences such as:

1.   Emotional Impact:

Negative conflict can have grave emotional impacts on your team members. It may frustrate them and make them feel empty. If the members feel that their opinions are going unheard, they become depressed and give up. Consequently, members become excessively strained, which adversely affects their personal and professional lives. Problems like lack of sleep, loss of appetite or overeating, headaches may arise in such a case.

2.   Decrease in Productivity:

Generally, negative conflict causes members to focus less on the problem at hand and more in gossiping and backbiting. When a major amount of time is spent in dealing with conflicts, members fail to focus on their task, which in turn leads to decreased productivity.

3.   Violence:

When negative conflicts go beyond the levels of resolution or escalates without mediation, intense situations may lead to violent behaviour, resulting in legal problems for the members as well as the organisation.

4.   Fatal Consequences:

When people are increasingly frustrated with the levels of conflict in the team or organisation, they may choose to leave it. Quitting of key members can be detrimental to the organisation's growth and development. Moreover, once members leave, the organisation has to incur additional costs of recruiting new members and training them. In extreme cases, it may risk dissolution or selling up.

Lehmann Brothers is one such firm, which had to face selling up because of negative conflicts. Within this firm, a severe conflict between the traders and the bankers led to the corporation's demise. There was no unified vision in the organisation. There was a common perception among the traders and the bankers that the other group was working towards fulfilling their separate objectives. Such a perception exaggerated the differences between the two groups. This creation of factions within the organisation proved detrimental to the organisation's overall performance, and eventually led to bankruptcy.

Conflict Management

We learned that conflicts could have both positive and negative impacts. This is where the concept of conflict management comes up. Conflict management is the process of balancing the conflicts in such a way that the negative conflicts are limited, while the positive conflicts are promoted. Conflict management aims to facilitate learning, and enhance group outcomes like effectiveness, efficiency, productivity, and performance.

> Conflict management is the process of balancing the conflicts in such a way that the negative conflicts are limited, while the positive conflicts are promoted.

Conflict management should aim for minimising negative conflicts at all levels and maintain a moderate amount of substantive conflicts.

To effectively implement conflict management strategies, one must satisfy the following criteria:

1. **Organisation Learning and Effectiveness:** In order to fulfil this requirement, conflict management should reinforce innovative ideas and encourage critical thinking.

2. **Identify the Needs:** Sometimes conflicts arise because of improper fulfilment of the members' needs. The management should concentrate on identifying these needs.

3. **Ethics:** A manager must behave ethically, and to do so, he/she must be open to new information and willing to adapt to change.

'AIMR' For Conflict Management

Conflict management is essentially to find out a solution that best fits the organisation's goals, but doesn't ignore the team members' perception of justice and fairness. When a conflict arises in your team, react to it by assessing the situation that led to it. Then proactively analyse the situation, until it fulfils all the requirements. Once you feel that all the team members have been justified, you should decide if this is a single-case conflict, or one that can be used as a prototype in the future. The process of conflict management starts on a reactive note, but towards the end, it becomes a proactive decision.

There are four steps of conflict management:

- **A – Anticipate**

Diligently collect information that can lead to conflict. Assess the information and develop strategies accordingly to prevent it. Ideally, it would be best if you involve your team in the process. This would effectively build an environment, where everyone is aware of how the conflict may arise, and therefore can proactively take steps to prevent it.

- **I – Identify**

When a conflict arises, take time to analyse the situation and identify the reasons behind it. Take into consideration the opinions of every individual in your team. This will give you fresh perspectives, allowing you to arrive at optimal solutions.

- **M – Manage**

Conflicts are emotional and should therefore be handled sensitively. Remember that every individual values his/her feelings more and hence the conflict should be managed in such a way that no one feels left out or hurt.

- **R – Resolve**

Always ensure that you are empathetic towards every member of the team. The solution of the conflict should be in the interests of the organisation, while at the same time, it should not disregard the team members' opinions and emotions.

Conflicts should be solution-driven – both creative and integrative. You should see to it that the conflicts give way to more insightful results, and are non-confrontational. Effective conflict management can go a long way in building a great rapport in your team and increasing productivity.

Chapter Rewind

- Without positive conflict, an organisation will fail to adapt to change and hence will stagnate.

- Positive conflict curbs groupthink and encourages application of creative thought processes and innovative ideas.

- Conflict management is essentially to find out a solution that best fits the organisation's goals, but doesn't ignore the team members' perception of justice and fairness.

- The process of conflict management starts on a reactive note, but towards the end, it becomes a proactive decision.

- Conflicts are emotional and should therefore be handled sensitively.

- Always ensure that you are empathetic towards every member of the team.

"Appreciate everything your associates do for the business. Nothing else can quite substitute for a few well chosen, well-timed, sincere works of praise. They're absolutely free and worth a fortune."

- Sam Walton

CHAPTER 10

REWARDING YOUR TEAM

The Special Day

Harry was a soft-spoken manager; he was quite popular in his organization. His team always achieved great performances that were appreciated by the clients. His team members also liked their cheerful and motivated manager.

When Harry's team came up with a tool that saved a considerable amount of the organization's expenses in marketing, their team got an onstage recognition in the annual event. Harry had made sure beforehand that all the team members' names are announced on the stage, and that each of them gets a gift of appreciation. This came as a surprise to the team members and their pleasure knew no bounds on receiving such special recognition.

More than just making his team members happy, Harry also indirectly motivated them by recognising their efforts.

Rise by Lifting Others

Rewarding your colleagues for their efforts, beyond their pay and benefits package builds trust and strengthens loyalty. Team rewards present a great opportunity to help foster team bonding. Here are some of the benefits of rewarding your team members.

1. Opens the Lines of Communication

Rewarding people by openly recognising their talents is a good way to engage conversation and build positive relationships.

2. Develops Trust

Trust is a critical issue when it comes to managing a team. Rewarding the team members for their genuine efforts lets them know how much you value them and tells them that their hard work isn't going unnoticed.

3. Encourages Loyalty

When people are genuinely appreciated, they become loyal to you and committed to go beyond the call of duty to reach the set goals. They strive to exceed their job expectations, and this spells productivity at the organisational level.

4. Boosts Morale

When team members' efforts are recognised, they feel good about their jobs and tend to become better at it. This boosts the team's morale and performance. On the other hand, it becomes quite a messy affair when the management does not properly appreciate the team's hard work. People stop caring and just put in their time, no effort.

5. Creates a Productive Environment

Recognition and appreciation improves the organisation's bottom line by creating a work environment where people do not shy away from giving their best. This will happen when people feel that their earnest efforts do not go unnoticed and contribute to the organisation's growth. Rewarding not only makes the team members feel good about themselves, but also motivates them to do better. A sincere "thank you" or a small reward for a job well done is appreciated and encourages people to repeat the good behaviour.

Adam's Equity Theory

John Stacey Adams, a workplace and behavioural psychologist, put forward the Equity Theory in 1963. It is one of the theories that explain the degree of satisfaction or dissatisfaction of employees on the basis of their perception of the distribution of resources. It proposes that individuals will experience distress or dissatisfaction when they perceive themselves to be under-rewarded or over-rewarded. This dissatisfaction of the individuals will lead them to put in efforts that will contribute to equity.

Adam's Definition of Equity

If an individual perceives the ratio of their inputs to their outcomes are equivalent to those around him/her, then they are in a state of equity. For example, let us compare two people, Lisa and Mark working together in an organisation. Lisa is a fresher and is paid less than Mark who has an experience of five years. Now, Lisa compares the ratio of her inputs to outcomes with that of Mark's as follows:

1. Lisa is a fresher – therefore, her inputs to the company are lesser than that of Mark's.

2. Because Lisa's inputs are lesser, the outcomes (salary and benefits) are lesser than that of Mark.

3. The ratios are equivalent and hence Lisa stays in a state of equity.

This can be illustrated by the following equation:

$$\frac{\text{Individual' s outcomes}}{\text{Individual' s own inputs}} = \frac{\text{Relational partner' s outcomes}}{\text{Relational partner' s inputs}}$$

Inputs and Outcomes

Inputs

Inputs are what the individual contributes to the team/organisation. The inputs can have a positive or a negative impact on the organisation, which will consequently translate to rewards or costs for the individual, respectively. Inputs typically include:

- Time
- Loyalty
- Commitment
- Adaptability
- Tolerance
- Enthusiasm
- Trust in Superiors
- Skill
- Effort
- Hard Work
- Ability
- Flexibility
- Determination
- Personal Sacrifice
- Peer Support

Outcomes

Outcomes are the positive or negative consequences that the individual gets from his/her job. Outcomes typically include:

- Financial rewards such as salary, benefits, perks, etc.
- Intangibles that typically include:
  - Recognition
  - Reputation
  - Responsibility
  - Sense of achievement
  - Praise
  - Stimulus
  - Sense of advancement/growth

♦ Job security

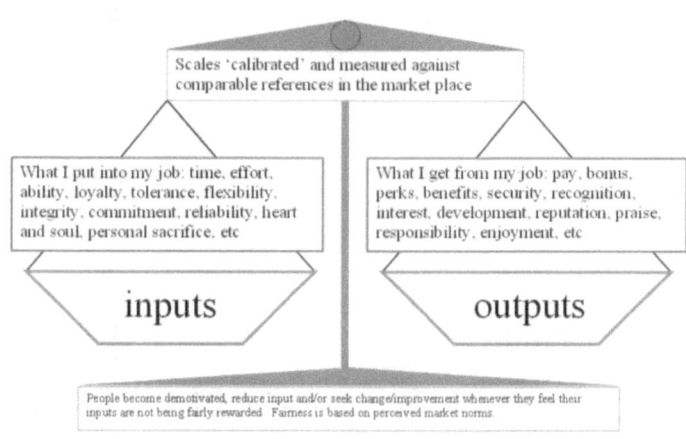

Adam's Equity Theory Diagram for Job Motivation

Significance

The Equity Theory is not merely an assessment of effort and reward. In fact, it goes beyond the assessment to add a crucial perspective of comparison with others. It explains why salary and benefits alone do not keep people satisfied. It says that we seek balance between what we put into the job and what we get out of it based on the comparison of our efforts and consequences with those of others, whom we consider as relevant reference points.

This means that our perception of equity does not depend on the ratio of inputs to outputs alone, it rather depends on how we see it with respect to referent others. Our perception of a fair ratio comes from a comparison of ourselves with others. Adam's Equity Theory is therefore more of a comprehensive motivational model, than an assessment theory of efforts and rewards.

The 'Right' to Reward

Consider a scenario where you decide to reward one of your team members for her exceptional efforts in designing an optimal business model. It is winter and so you present a turkey to her that she can enjoy with her family and friends. She smiles, thanks you politely, and instantly puts the turkey in the office refrigerator. You are happy because you think you aptly rewarded her for her efforts and she is happy because her hard work was properly appreciated. Or was it?

Things aren't always as they appear. You never took time to learn that she is a vegan. You didn't know that she commutes an hour to the office by bus, and the turkey will go all drippy and soggy by the time she can drop it at a friend's house.

It is important that you reward your team members for their effort, but it is equally important to take the time to learn what your team members really want as rewards. However, that too isn't always possible. Therefore, the quintessential question arises. How to reward your team members? How to recognise their efforts in a manner that they appreciate your polite gesture? Here is how:

1.   Say Thank You

The least thing you can do is saying thank you. It passes on a message that you have recognised good performance. For many, that is enough to motivate and encourage. Agreed that they work for pay, but it always feels

> A sincere thank you, combined with a polite smile can do wonders to the individual's motivation level.

good when some extra appreciation comes along. A sincere thank you, combined with a polite smile can do wonders to the individual's motivation level. Not just routine comments – rather go out of your way and thank your team members whenever you notice them doing something you appreciate.

Give sincere feedback about what they have done and how it has contributed, and share the achievement with your team. In the process, don't hesitate to point out the negative aspects. That will only hamper better performance. In fact, pointing where they have fallen short while appreciating their good efforts can act as a morale booster.

Celebrate and share success. Don't wait to praise an individual until you are alone with him/her. Find an opportunity when they are with their colleagues and praise them. It will mean a lot and create a buzz.

2.   Don't Handpick

Agreed that it is nice to recognise the top performers, but you don't want it to seem like you are being partial, or playing favourites. Be objective while placing rewards – it will establish a reward system based on hard results. For example, present an award on the basis of least number of project errors, maximum sales, etc. This will be a fair approach and boost a competitive spirit among others.

3.   The Personal Touch

They all know you as their manager. You can be a little bit personal with them while rewarding. It will be endearing and they will get to know you better. For example, find out about their hobbies and interests, and pick up something that has to do with the particular interest whenever you find an opportunity to do so. Everyone likes it when his or her manager says, "I really appreciate what you do, and I got this for you as a small token." It may not cost much, but the thought it evokes will make a lot of difference.

4.   Take Them for a Treat

An occasional treat always does wonders. It is a great opportunity to get to know each other informally, which in turn will strengthen the bond of trust and loyalty in your team. In case your team has worked long or unsociable hours that had an impact on their personal lives, extend the treat to be shared with their loved ones as well. It shows your appreciation for their efforts and makes them feel good about their job as well.

5.   Time Off

Some free time can be the most valuable gift for some people. Allowing flexibility in work hours, or giving them a day off when possible, may work wonders for their motivation and confidence levels.

6.   Encourage Healthy Competition

Hosting a friendly workplace competition is a great way to build productivity and encourage a greater sense of community among the team members. Announce the competition as well as the prizes beforehand, to buzz up the excitement levels, and to give them an early idea of what is at stake. A healthy competition will foster great team spirit and relationships among the team members, which is a good thing, because you will then get more collaborative efforts leading to enhanced productivity.

Giving out awards for their efforts can also work miracles for the team spirits. They don't have to win the awards; just a nomination can thrust enough drive to perform better. This will also foster a healthy competitive spirit in the team.

7.   Offer Development Opportunities

Development opportunities do not only mean promotions. It is one of the intentions of course, but not the only one. Development's main intention should be to make people the best they can be at their jobs. And who hates a promotion per se?

Take time to identify people's strengths and assign work accordingly, whenever such an opportunity presents itself. Delegate some of your responsibilities to the team. It will have a positive impact on their performance and self-confidence. They will appreciate the fact that you have recognised what they are good at.

Chapter Rewind

- Reward with consent.

- Always try to bring the group together while rewarding.

- Go out of your way sometimes to make them feel special.

- Do not only think of rewards as money – people appreciate non-monetary perks too.

- Avoid being biased towards individual performances as much as possible; focus on the team accomplishments.

- Do not reward your team with something that doesn't have a collective value for a team accomplishment.